Katarina's Return

THE SHADOWDANCE CLUB 1

AVERY GALE®

DEDICATION

To Cathy and Karen...

We are cousins by birth, but best friends by choice. Without your never-ending encouragement and unfailing support, this book would have never seen the light of day.

Thank you from the bottom of my heart.

Chapter 1

ALEX AND ZACH Lamont usually used a pickup or small ATV to check the perimeter fence, but had opted to use horses today, hoping for a bit of stealth. There had been a security breach near the small lake at the back of their property the night before, but they'd been too busy at ShadowDance to check it out. The brothers had named their BDSM club after the ranch their father had built years before.

Honoring his Native American ancestry, Daniel Lamont had called his mountain retreat and hobby ranch ShadowDance. The local elders told stories of their forefathers' respect for the mountain and how the spirits loved dancing with the shadows in the forest that blankets the entire area. And, despite their years traveling the world while in the military, the ranch had always held a special place in Alex and Zach's hearts. The small lake's remote location made it a rendezvous hotspot for local, young romantics and while they appreciated their need for privacy, the Lamonts and their ranch hands were getting tired of repairing the damage to the fencing and cleaning up the aftermath of the lovers' liaisons. It was just after daybreak, so with a little luck, they just might be early enough catch their 'guests' unaware and have a chance to discourage any future visits.

Since starting The ShadowDance Club seven years ago, it had become wildly successful. Its secluded location and reputation for discretion made it a safe haven for BDSM enthusiasts from all over the nation. Weeklong training classes, catering to both beginners and those in long-term D/s relationships, had long waiting lists, and since those visitors brought a lot of business to the local hotels and restaurants, The Club, as it was referred to locally, enjoyed the full support of the community, most of whom were long-time members.

Climax, Colorado, was a community like no other. Its residents were holdovers from another era. Most were either flower children of the '70s free spirits or their children, so "live and let live" was not just a motto, but a creed all the townspeople lived by.

Hoping for a chance to enjoy the view and recharge a bit, Alex and Zach rode in silence. If last night's alarm had occurred during a Club event, it wouldn't have mattered how inconvenient checking would be, the safety of their members was always their priority. The Club's background checks done on all members and staff rivaled those for top government posts. A military-trained security staff, and a top-of-the-line surveillance system also worked to make The ShadowDance Club a secure place to explore a sexual lifestyle which followed the 'Safe, Sane, and Consensual' model for BDSM play. Club members ran the full gambit, from weekend players to twenty-four seven sex slaves, and that variety ensured there was always something interesting happening at The Club.

Putting the finishing touches on an upcoming 'Beach Party' was taking a toll on Alex and Zach as well as their staff. The details for this event, which would showcase their extensive remodeling and additional play areas, had been staggering. The logistical challenges alone had been mind-boggling. First, several truckloads of pure white sand that would be the envy of South Beach, Florida had been stuck on a mountain switchback for hours before they'd been able to get experienced drivers in place who could move the trucks safely up and over the mountain. Then, after a night on the town, the waterfall sculptor fell off the enormous stone structure he'd been creating.

The sculptor's broken ankle put him out of commission, and the search for a replacement who could pass their security checks and was willing to come sooner than the usual four-to-six-month wait had been mighty expensive. Their staff was top-notch, but dealing with outsiders had left them all feeling like they'd been scrambling for months. Things had finally started to fall into place, and it looked like it would be smooth sailing as soon as they explained to the trespassing Romeo and Juliet the lake was off-limits.

Echo Lake was aptly named because the rock walls along the backside of the water amplified even the smallest sound. It was easily accessible from the house and The Club, but not many people knew how to make their way along the complicated trails through the forests covering much of the mountain, and even fewer would know how to do so undetected.

There were only ten or eleven people who would be able to find the small brush-covered entrance through the rock wall along the small meadow by the lake. Figuring they'd be dealing with either adults or kids they already knew, both Alex and Zach felt it best to handle the situation personally. Even though they shared Special Forces military backgrounds with their security staff, the Lamonts had spent the majority of their childhood in Climax and understood the importance of handling certain situations with a bit more finesse than some of their staff.

Winding their way through the short canyon and moving along the edge of the river that fed the lake, they set a steady pace, enjoying the early morning sounds, and didn't feel any need to fill the silence. But soon the sounds of soft cries and muffled moans filled the air. These were not the moans of a submissive's pleasure, these were sounds of genuine pain. Both Alex and Zach were experienced Doms, they could easily recognize the difference between a woman's sounds of pleasure driven by erotic pain and the cries of injury-induced pain. Picking up their pace, they moved quickly through the trees, trying to maintain their cover while still looking out over the lake. What they saw brought them to a dead stop.

KATARINA MCKAY HAD finally managed to crawl out of the frigid water but couldn't get her abused muscles to move any farther. Moaning, she lay at the edge of the lake's crystal-clear water, hoping the first rays of the midsummer sunlight would soak in and ease her pain and exhaustion. She'd driven for hours, fighting to hold on to her last remnants of strength and fight against the pain. She'd known there was only one place she'd be able to feel truly safe. Now, she was fighting to stay awake, knowing she needed to get back to the small hiding place she'd taken shelter in late last night. Staying out of sight was a priority, but when the pain had finally overwhelmed her, she'd crawled to the water, letting it sooth the deep lashes on her back and legs.

Kat had always planned to return home, but this was

not the way any of those fantasies had played out in her mind. She was surprised, but grateful the Lamont brothers had decided to sand the edge of the lake. All her memories of the lake included its rocky shore, the jagged black rocks were always such a sharp contrast to the pristine crystal-blue water. Lying on the soft sand in the warm sunlight, Kat promised herself she would close her eyes for just a few minutes. With a sigh of exhaustion, Katarina let her eyes drift closed as the pain free darkness washed over her.

ALEX AND ZACH only paused for a heartbeat before spurring their horses and taking off at a dead run around the lake.

"What the hell?" Zach couldn't believe what he was seeing. "Is that a woman? And Christ Almighty, are those whiplashes? Get Colt on the phone. Get help headed this way."

Zach had already dug his heels into his horse's sides and was skirting the lake's sanded edge. He could hear Alex barking commands, but was ignoring them because there was something hauntingly familiar about the woman lying on her side, facing away from the water's edge. Even though she was angled away from his approach, he knew, just knew it was her, the one woman they'd let slip through their fingers. He leapt off his horse before it had even come to a full stop and was kneeling beside the naked woman when Alex approached on the other side.

"Is she alive?" Alex asked, kneeling beside her while Zach picked up her wrist, checking her pulse.

"Her pulse is awfully weak, but it's there. You make the calls, make sure they bring my bag and have them get the paramedics and the sheriff headed this way. We've got to figure out how to get her out of here without doing any further damage." Zach had been the medic for their teams in the military. He knew he was the logical choice to provide care; he also knew the minute Alex figured out it was Kat, everything was going to change, and his brother's rational decision-making skills were going to be for shit.

Alex was known for his steely, always-in-control personality. He was widely respected as the one who could always be counted on to make decisions based on facts. He carefully weighed options and calculated probabilities in the time it took most people to blink. But Katarina McKay had always been the one weak spot in Alex's perfectly ordered world.

Brushing her matted hair back from her face, Alex paled and froze. "Oh my God, Katarina." There was a split second when Zach thought his brother was going to go right over the edge into insanity. Alex's eyes widened, his breathing stopped, and he looked as if he'd seen a ghost, but then he shifted into full boss mode. Opening his phone, Alex began barking orders to Colt Matthews, who'd been their chief of security since they'd opened The Club.

Colt Matthews had been their team leader during each tour of duty. There simply wasn't anyone better at his job than Colt. The man was an electronics whiz extraordinaire, a master at anticipating every possible scenario then strategizing responses, and he was the closest thing they'd ever had to a best friend. They'd entrusted their lives to Colt too many times to count and would trust him with their younger sister's life if the two could ever stop bickering long enough to recognize their mutual attraction.

Finishing up his call and returning to Kat's side, Alex asked, "Who the fuck do you think did this to her? And why is she out here alone in the middle of nowhere? Why didn't she call us? Why didn't she come to the house? Christ, how did she even make it this far?" Kat's soft moan brought Alex's attention back to her and the current situation. He ran soothing touches down her soft cheeks, murmuring to her to hang in there, letting her know help was on the way, while Zach tried to assess her injuries.

Zach covered her with a light foil blanket from the first aid kit he always carried in his saddlebags. In only a few minutes, Zach knew there would be people everywhere, and the fewer people who saw who he considered *theirs* the better. Knowing they didn't really have a claim to Kat, yet, didn't matter because they would soon. She wasn't slipping through their fingers again.

Suddenly, the quiet was shattered as SUVs came barreling around the lake. Colt's custom-built ATV slid to a stop, and the paramedics jumped out of the enclosed unit before it even stopped rolling. While they worked to stabilize Kat, a backup team immediately began securing the area. Since no one knew the circumstances of her arrival, every precaution for her safety would be taken. In twenty minutes, she had been stabilized, IVs started, and was being loaded into the ATV.

KAT FELT LIKE she was lost in a thick fog. She could hear voices, but everything felt like it was just out of her reach. The sounds began to swirl closer until she heard a voice say, "What hospital are you taking her to?" That voice... she knew it... she was sure she did. Where was she? The last thing she remembered was the cool water. Echo Lake.

She was by Alex and Zach's family's mountain lake. That was Alex's voice. *Hospital? Oh God! No!*

Kat came up fighting, struggling to sit up. She managed to scramble off the gurney while the paramedics were too startled by her sudden movements to stop her. Spinning around to see what the commotion was, Alex's sharp voice sounded above all the others.

"Katarina! Stop! Now!"

In the deepest part of her mind, she recognized and responded to the authority of a Dom and froze. Even after all she'd been through at the hands of a ruthless sadist, her soul recognized the unyielding command. Kat stood absolutely still clutching the blanket around her. She swayed once before her knees gave out, collapsing just as Zach wrapped his arms around her battered body. Scooping her up, Zach held her against his chest as she cried softly, pleading. "Please, please, please…"

"Please what, kitten? Tell me what you need." Zach's soft words whispered against her hair. He couldn't know the calm his embrace brought to her. "Tell me who hurt you, baby. Let us fix this for you. Let us take care of you."

Looking up into his face, she spoke in a broken sob. "Please, Zach, don't let them take me. No hospitals, no doctors. He'll know, he'll find me. If my name appears anywhere, he'll know, and he'll come and finish what he started." Kat knew he could hear the fear in her voice, but there wasn't any way to avoid it.

Her trembling started at her core and spread outward until Zach had to tighten his hold to keep her from shaking right out of his arms. Kat's eyes closed slowly as she let herself relax into the safety that had always been Zachary Lamont. He had always been her white knight, and she knew he would protect her with his life. With his warmth surrounding her, she let the darkness take her once again.

Chapter 2

Alex stood in the doorway and wondered for the hundredth time how long a person could sleep. He and Zach had taken turns sleeping in the chair beside Kat's bed for nearly twenty-four straight hours, and she'd barely stirred. Katarina had finally fallen into a fitful sleep after Doc Woods stitched up the worst of the lashes on her back and carefully treated all the other wounds. She had only slept peacefully when either Alex or Zach kept her hand held securely in theirs. Even in her sleep, she trusted them. Each time they'd try to leave her alone, she had quickly become agitated. Whatever filled her nightmares caused agonized screams and pleading sobs that only seemed to settle if they were nearby.

"Did you ever think we'd get a second chance?" Zach's quiet inquiry told Alex his brother had felt him approach even though Alex knew he hadn't made a sound. Their twin bond had always been particularly strong. More often than not, it had been to their mutual benefit, but on rare occasions, it was damned unhandy. Both Zach and Alex had discovered early in life, knowing what another person is thinking and feeling all the time made it very difficult to define yourself. Individuality had sometimes been a hard-won battle. It had taken them years to accept their differences, to feel secure enough to allow those traits to complement each other and work together.

Alex sighed and walked farther into the room. Coming up on the other side of the bed, he leaned against the warm glass of the window and looked out over the gardens behind The Club. It was early afternoon, and the shadows were slowly creeping across the back acreage. The entire area would soon become a wonderland of twinkling lights, highlighting the vine-covered walkways and secluded hiding spots once darkness fell. Alex stood watching Katarina sleep for a few moments before looking up at Zach to respond.

"No. I was afraid we'd lost her forever. I'd wanted to believe we'd get another chance, but as the years went by, I lost hope. I didn't really believe fate would give me the opportunity to make it up to her, hell, to either of you." Blowing out an exhausted breath, Alex continued, "You lost her and missed her every bit as much or perhaps even more than I did, and the loss wasn't by your own actions, yet you never blamed me. Even now, I'm humbled by that fact."

Zach's eyes never left Kat's soft face. In sleep she looked like an angel, her soft blonde curls fanned out over the pillow like a halo. Her skin had always reminded him of the finest porcelain, smooth and so white, it almost glowed. Even marred by bruises, her beauty was heart-stopping. Speaking softly, Zach said, "It wasn't our time, but it is now." He paused for several long seconds before speaking more forcefully. "We have to make her see that, brother. In her heart, she knows she is safe here, this is where she belongs, she belongs to us. We'll fix this. We have to do whatever it takes to make sure the bastard who did this never gets another shot. Fuck, we have to make sure he never hurts any woman. Christ, Alex, did you see, *really see*, what he did to her? That perfectly spaced slicing is the work of a well-practiced sadist. This isn't the work of a true Dom or at least not one who would ever be allowed at ShadowDance."

"Agreed. It's a violation of trust on so many levels. Katarina's heart is going to be very fragile, and rebuilding her trust will take time, but the fact she felt safe enough to return and hide out here gives me hope." Alex sat and watched Katarina for several long moments before speaking again, "I won't let either of you down again, I swear it. We'll work it out this time. She needs us. She may not want to admit it yet, but she will." Alex's wistful tone was such a contrast to his Dom persona, it caused Zach to glance up to ensure the words really had come from his take-no-prisoners brother. Alex's eyes were a softer brown than Zach had seen them since Kat had left.

She'd been so young and so sure she understood what they wanted from her, and they'd been equally convinced she would be disillusioned if she'd known the stark reality of their lives. They'd been real bastards, trying to save her from them. As long as he lived, he'd never forget looking up to see her standing in that doorway, even with the harsh light streaming in from behind her, making her wild mane of blonde curls glow. He'd watched as the fire and light in her eyes had faded and then finally been extinguished. The look of utter defeat and disgust haunted him still.

"Zach?" Kat's soft whisper brought him out of the tortured memory and back to the only woman he and his brother had ever truly loved.

"YES, KITTEN. I'M here. We're both here." Zach's words passed over her face like a gentle breeze. He smelled of soap, mint, and Zach. He'd leaned close to her to speak, then let his lips pass over the shell of her ear in a soft caress meant to sooth and comfort, but Kat felt the familiar tightening in her lower body. The tingling sparks only the Lamont brothers had ever been able to ignite within her felt new, but at the same time held a peaceful familiarity. In that moment, Kat knew she had finally made it home.

Letting the lull of safety wash over her, she knew, deep in her heart, it wouldn't last, she couldn't stay because it wouldn't be fair to them. But in this moment, she was truly safe. That feeling of safety was almost a narcotic, it would be addictive, and Kat knew she would have to move on as soon as she was able. She also knew they would use their considerable resources to protect her, so until she was well enough to disappear again, she would stay. The challenge would be to not lose her heart to them... again.

ALEX WATCHED HIS brother with Katarina and felt as if the whole world shifted then stilled. For just those few brief seconds all had been right in his world. He didn't know why the Universe was giving him this second chance, but he was going to find a way to make sure Kat understood the three of them belonged together. He and Zach had always known they would share a woman. It wasn't a decision they'd made consciously, it had just always been a given. Alex had been such a fool, he had ignored all the signs, and it wasn't until Katarina had left them that they'd known for sure she was the one.

Marriage in Climax was not defined as narrowly as it was in other places. There were as many reasons the locals chose to share a woman as there were pluralistic couples, but once those relationships were formed, they lasted a lifetime. Infidelity was uncommon and never tolerated, and abuse of any woman or child was dealt with swiftly. Protecting their women was the duty and honor of each man in their close-knit community. The care, protection, and satisfaction of the women were always first and foremost in every decision. Often visitors to their community commented on how happy the women appeared. It wasn't just an appearance, it was a fact, and it certainly wasn't an accident.

Stepping forward, Alex said, "Zach, go get something to eat. Get some rest. I'll sit with her. She's going to need you when she wakes up."

"I don't want to leave her, she's so fragile," Zach said, brushing his knuckles across her lips as he spoke.

"She'll be fine. I'll call you if she wakes. I want us to begin as we intend to go, and that means she needs to deal with us both. We both know she craves my dominance, but will seek shelter in you if we allow it." Alex had always been the more Alpha of the two of them. His no-nonsense approach was softened by Zach's more laid-back way of dealing with people, and that combination had made them effective soldiers and wildly successful businessmen. But anyone mistaking Zachary Lamont as a pushover would quickly see the error of that assessment. They were both Doms to their core. There was a long-standing joke among the other Doms at The Club that said, the only real difference between them was in their 'communication style.'

They were mirror images of one another, easily passing

for each other, and most people had to actually talk to them in order to know which brother they were dealing with. Both were imposing figures, standing six-two with broad shoulders and deep, muscular chests that were well defined by long hours spent in the gym. Their ink black hair, dark eyes, and golden tan skin highlighted their Native American heritage. It didn't take long in a conversation to know whether you were dealing with demanding Alex or the cajoling Zach. Their younger sister, Jenna, was the only one who never mixed them up, and she'd spoiled a lot of their fun over the years with her ability to tell them apart even at a distance.

ALEX SAT ON the bed beside Katarina, softly stroking the side of her face, talking to her as if she were a small child he'd been watching sleep. She looked like a petite, fallen angel, battered and bruised, but still maintaining an innocence that called to him. Letting his mind drift back to the last time he'd seen her set off spikes of pain lancing through his chest. He'd known she wasn't ready for them, but she'd been so stubborn and sure. So, he'd made certain she'd gotten a chance to really see them in action.

The fallout had been so much greater than he'd ever dreamed it might be. Rather than just pushing her to understand why she needed to wait, live her life, experience everything that could be found outside of Climax before 'settling down' with them, she'd totally misunderstood the play scene she'd walked in on. The BDSM scene they'd planned had been with a woman whose pleasure could only be found through a deeper edge of pain, and they'd been happy to oblige her. They'd become caught up in the scene and so arrogant in their expectation of Kat's reaction, they'd completely forgotten about her family history of domestic violence. It had been a catastrophic and unforgivable miscalculation on their part.

Instead of pushing her to understand, they had inadvertently scared her right out of their lives. Katarina had opened the door of their dungeon just as the last lash of his single-tail whip had taken the woman over the edge into a screaming orgasm. It had only taken Kat seconds to take in what she believed was abuse and run. Her memories of her mother's long line of abusive relationships had triggered a panic they had naively never considered a possibility. By the time they had provided aftercare for their sub, Katarina had fled The Club. By the next morning, her small apartment was empty, and she'd disappeared from their lives... until yesterday.

Where had she gone? They'd searched for her and had also hired others to look, but it was as if she'd just vanished into the night. They'd put considerable pressure on Jenna who had always been Katarina's best friend. They'd demanded answers, but she had steadfastly insisted she didn't know where her best friend might have gone. Jenna had always held them responsible for Kat's leaving, and Alex had no doubt their relationship with their younger sister had suffered as a result.

He planned to find out how Katarina had just disappeared without a trace. Hiding is never easy; even when you were trained in covert operations and knew what you were doing, it was damned difficult. The failure rate of individuals in witness protection programs was testimony of just how difficult it was to truly become someone else. Hell, she hadn't had any resources or training, and still, she had successfully eluded them.

How had she allowed herself to become involved with someone who would abuse her trust and her body so badly? How had she gotten away from him and what kind of danger was she still in? It was going to be very difficult to go slowly when, in his heart, Alex knew the clock was ticking. That gut-level alarm system had saved his ass way too many times to ignore it now. Watching her, he wished she would just wake up and talk to them.

Chapter 3

KATARINA HAD ALWAYS had trouble waking up, but this felt different, it was more like being trapped inside a bubble that was slowly trying to drift to the surface, fighting to make its way through muddy water. She could hear people speaking, but their voices seemed muffled and distant. She ached all over. God, everything ached. What the hell had she done?

Keeping her eyes closed, she tried to piece together the snippets of information she could remember. She sure remembered the scene at that club in Las Vegas. Holy shit, how had she gotten herself into such a mess? And she remembered the woman who helped her escape; she really needed to check on Mia. Not many people would have taken that risk, and Kat wanted to make sure Mia hadn't suffered for being such a brave good Samaritan.

She remembered driving all night to get away, making sure she got as far as away as possible from Cal. Kat knew without any doubt, getting involved with Calvin Robertson was the single worst decision she'd ever made. He had seemed so perfect in the beginning, good-looking in a Vogue-meets-Dark-Shadows kind of way, successful, great family connections, and he shared her interest in BDSM. He'd said he was willing to "teach her everything she needed to know" to be the perfect submissive. He'd even agreed to her 'no penetrative sex' rule until she was trained, at which time, he'd said they would renegotiate their time together. She had never intended to change her mind, but she hadn't bothered to tell him that part. The whole idea of being trained to be a sub had sounded like a good deal…but the reality had been far more menacing.

Giving herself a mental slap to refocus, she remembered hiding her car in the trees and making her way to the lake. And she was pretty sure she remembered hearing Alex's voice, being held by Zach, and feeling sad because she'd known she'd have to leave again soon. But that was the last thing she remembered.

Moving her fingers, she felt sheets which were obviously not her usual Walmart-knock-off version of fine linen and warm callused fingers. *What the hell?* Struggling to get her eyes open and blinking against the brightness, Kat saw Alex gazing at her with a soft look of expectation. There was that sexy half smile she'd seen in almost every dream she'd had since she'd become best friends with Jenna in elementary school. God, how she'd missed them.

"Hello there, beautiful. Welcome back to the land of the conscious. We've been waiting for you to open those gorgeous blue eyes," Alex spoke softly.

Kat knew too well it wasn't his usual tone. This version of Alex was comforting and sweet, but it wasn't the run-to-the-roar Alex she'd fallen in love with as a child and had never been able to put out of her mind. That Alex was well used to giving orders and having them followed immediately. Yes, that Alex was a Dom through and through.

Alex's deep voice brought her mind back into focus. "Zach will be here in just a minute. I sent him a text when I felt you starting to stir."

"How long have I been sleeping? Can I get a drink of

water?" Kat's throat felt like it was lined with sandpaper, and she hoped the water would help clear the cobwebs in her mind. She sipped at the cool water from the cup Alex held up to her parched lips and fought the temptation to gulp it all at one time. Groaning inwardly, Kat could only imagine how she must look. "I'm sorry I've been so much trouble. I promise to be out of your way just as soon as I can get some clothes and get back to my car."

Alex just watched her, and if she hadn't known him so well, she might have missed the slight tightening of his jaw before it relaxed again. He wasn't happy with what she'd said, and she'd known he wouldn't be, but that was just too bad.

It wouldn't be safe for her to be here, and they'd had their chance seven years ago. They hadn't wanted her then, and she wasn't going to stick around to give them another shot at destroying what little pride she'd been able to salvage the last time. Damn and double damn, the huge target she'd managed to paint on her back would keep her on the move for years if not forever. She was just so tired and sad. How had her life spiraled out of control again after years of piecing together her heart and building a new life for herself? It would be so nice to just let go and let someone else take care of things, but she would never ask them to risk the trouble she was sure to have following her.

Alex's steady gaze was starting to unnerve her, but she wasn't going to let him know it. Alex and Zach both favored their father, and owing to Daniel Lamont's Native American heritage, their eyes were so dark, it was often difficult to discern the slight shift in the depth of the color depending on their mood. They had hair the color of coal which was always so shiny; Kat had often wondered if it was as soft as it looked.

"You've been sleeping for a little over twenty-four hours," Alex answered, after what seemed like several long minutes. "I don't even want to think about how exhausted you had to have been. We'll be discussing the importance of taking proper care of yourself, among other things, when you're feeling better. For now, let's concentrate on getting you freshened up, then getting you something to eat. How's that sound?" The answering growl of Kat's stomach kept her from denying how hungry she was. Frowning, Alex asked her, "When did you last eat?"

Oh boy, that sounded a lot more like the Alex she remembered. He seemed to be trying to hold Master Alex on a tight rein, so this probably wouldn't be a good time to push him by dodging his question.

"Well, um, today's Friday, right?" Kat inquired, then winced at Alex's thunderous expression.

Alex's brows knitted together, and he was growling under his breath. The only thing she heard was a snarly "Jesus" before Zach came through the door, saving Kat from having to deal with the decidedly crankier Alex.

"KITTEN, YOU'RE AWAKE! How are you feeling, darlin'? God, we've been so worried about you." Zach sat on the edge of the bed, holding her hand, and running the backs of his knuckles softly down the side of her cheek. Without meaning to, Kat leaned in to his touch, taking comfort in it even when she knew she should try to keep some distance between them. "You ready to get up out of that bed and take a shower? We tried to get as much of the pond water off you as we could, but Doc Woods didn't really want to share you so much." Zach grinned at her, his eyes alight with mischief.

"Doc Woods?" Kat groaned. "He won't tell anybody about me, will he? God, if he lets anyone know he's seen me... Damn, I gotta get out of here. He'll come here. You don't know how dangerous he is. It won't be safe for you. I can't stay. Where are my clothes?" Kat was near panic mode, trying very hard to not hyperventilate. By the time she stopped for a breath, she was frantically looking around for something to wear. She started to throw the sheet off until she realized she was naked beneath it. Damn, what has she been thinking laying on the beach naked? She didn't even want to consider who all had seen her.

"Whoa, kitten, slow down and take a breath. Christ, you're going to pull out all the stitches Doc worked so hard on. You know nobody's going to be able to pry information out of that old fart, hell, he didn't want to even talk to us about your condition." Zach had both his large hands on either side of her face, his nose nearly touching her own. "Breathe with me, kitten." Zach's entire focus was centered on her eyes. "That's it. In slowly, now out. In, now out. No, stop... Focus... That's it. In, now out. Stay with me, it'll be okay. You know you'll always be safe here."

She tried, she really did. Dammit, she didn't want to cry, but once the first tears broke over the lower rim of her eyes and rolled down her face, she broke into gut-wrenching sobs. Kat let herself fall in to the arms of the man who had always been her safety net. Zach pulled her close and held her, letting her release all the pent-up anxiety. He seemed to know they wouldn't be able to get any information until she was able to purge all the fear she was obviously guarding so closely.

Chapter 4

A LEX LEANED AGAINST the doorframe, trying to look casual when he felt anything but calm. *Just give me a name, Katarina, and I'll destroy the bastard who has done this to you. There won't be a hole deep enough for him to hide in, I promise you that.* He didn't speak, he didn't blink, he just watched. Everything about her drew him like a magnet to steel.

There was something almost mystical about the way she looked at him as if she could see all the way to the depths of his soul. It should have been unnerving, hell, it had been damned unsettling when he was younger. But the years have a way of making people more comfortable in their own skin, and he and his twin were very comfortable in theirs. Everything always came down to one simple word, *trust*. They had to gain Katarina's trust before they could help her recognize that they didn't plan to let her slip away again. But her immediate safety was going to have to be a priority for now. They needed to get her healthy and out of danger, then begin the long process of rebuilding what he'd so carelessly destroyed years ago.

As her sobs slowed until all he heard was little hiccups, Alex pushed away from the doorway and moved toward the bed.

"Let's get you up and into a nice warm shower. We'll

both help you get cleaned up and fed, and then we'll sit down and talk."

"Okay, if you could just point me to the bathroom and leave me something to wear, I'll join you when I'm finished." Kat held tightly to the sheet wrapped around her and began backing away from Zach. She was attempting to cover her breasts after the smooth cotton had slipped to her waist during her meltdown. Zach gently moved her hand to the side, slowly shaking his head at her efforts.

"Don't ever hide your body from us, kitten. You are beautiful, we will always enjoy seeing you. And we'll want access to what belongs to us." Putting a finger to her lips when she would have protested, Zach continued. "Don't try to deny what we all know is true. Whether you want to acknowledge it now or not, you are ours. We'll work it all out, don't worry. Now, let's get you up and into the shower."

Alex was already starting to unbutton his shirt and kicked off his shoes on the other side of the room, capturing Kat's attention. She could feel her breathing speed up, her breaths becoming much shallower, and she knew her pussy was most certainly becoming damp. Damn, her body was going to betray her if she didn't get them out of here quickly.

"I can take my own shower. You two surely have other things to do besides play nursemaid to me." Kat knew the squeak in her voice betrayed her nervousness thinking about being in the shower with Alex and Zach. Holy shit, she needed to focus on figuring out a way to keep the two of them from stealing her heart. But being naked with them, watching bubbles trail down broad, bronze, toned chests was going to be deliciously distracting. *Oh yeah, Kat, those thoughts are going to be really helpful.*

Good grief, what had she been thinking coming back to Climax? Alex and Zach were just too much for her to deal with… hell, they always had been. What had ever made her think she'd be able to resist the sin on a stick times two that was the Lamont twins was a mystery for sure.

"Is Jenna around? She could help me." Kat knew her words sounded lame. Damn and double damn, she sounded pathetic even to her own ears.

"I don't think so, Katarina." Alex smiled down at her. "You know the way it'll be with us. Don't even think anyone else is going to be taking care of you. Now be a good girl, and do as you're told. Let's get you on your feet and see how you do standing up." Alex stood at the edge of the bed, his bare chest mesmerizing her. God, he was even hotter now than he'd been when she was just a teenager who hadn't really seen any boys besides Alex and Zach. They'd always been so gorgeous, it should have almost been illegal. "Give me your hand, baby. Let me help you stand."

While Alex helped Kat slowly stand up from the edge of the bed, Zach moved to the side of the large room and began undressing. Sighing, Kat closed her eyes, trying to block out the fantasy that kept playing on a loop through her mind. Her imagination was working overtime, flashing pictures of the two of them sandwiching her between them, naked, wet, touching her everywhere… *Damn it, Kat, get a fucking grip and focus.* Trying not to wince as she straightened, she had to take a couple of deep breaths to ward off the dizziness and pain. She was finally able to get her shaky legs to cooperate and her feet to start moving forward.

Alex watched the expressions chase across Katarina's face—first resignation, then fear, followed closely by a flash of lust. Each emotion was there and then gone in the blink of an eye. He watched the pulse at the base of her neck speed up as her breathing became faster and shallower. Her eyes had dilated until they showed only a small ring of the clear blue that had always reminded him of the crystalline waters of the Caribbean Sea.

Wrapping his arm around her waist and keeping a tight hold on her arm, Alex watched her try to fight back the pain showing in the strain around her eyes and the thinning of her lush lips. God, she was still the most beautiful woman he'd ever seen. Even with all the marks another man had left to mar her perfect skin, Alex couldn't see anything but a glow that had always shone from deep within her. It didn't burn as bright as it once had, but he would make it his life's mission to bring it back and make sure it was never dimmed again.

Zach moved around them into the en suite bathroom which had been specially built for the woman they planned to share their lives with. Both he and Alex had always dreamed it would be Kat, but as the years had passed without them being able to find even a trace of her where-abouts, they'd simply kept the door closed at this end of the hall and tried to block out their tattered dream. Selita, their housekeep and cook, insisted on keeping fresh linens and flowers in the suite. Ever the romantic optimist, she had always sworn to them that "Miss Kat would come home." Groaning inwardly at that thought, Zach knew there would be simply no living with Selita now, she was never going to let them forget that she'd been right.

THEY'D GIVEN KAT a few minutes of privacy, but didn't stay out of the room long, fearing she wasn't as stable as she wanted to believe.

"Geez, can't you give a girl a chance to at least use the bathroom alone? This is embarrassing," Kat said as she reached over to flush the toilet.

"There's nothing to be embarrassed about, Katarina. We don't want you to lose your balance and fall. It would be easy to become light-headed after lying down for so long. You already have more than enough to recover from, let's not add a concussion to that list, shall we?" Alex's voice was a mixture of mellow caretaker and bossy Dom that had Kat grinning inwardly despite her annoyance with their intrusion. It sure hadn't taken Master Alex long to reappear.

The shower was huge—it was basically a room with warm brown tile covering the floor and a small bench. The walls were made of natural stone, and water poured from showerheads disguised to look like mini waterfalls all around the enclosure. The entire front of the shower was glass, ensuring anyone in the bathroom had a front-row seat to any 'water sports' taking place in the shower. *Oh yeah, this shower was definitely designed for group activities.*

Stepping under the spray, Kat leaned her head back and sighed, just enjoying the feel of the warm water caressing her breasts and stomach. Yes, the Lamonts had always known how to live right. Their parents had been wealthy beyond her imagination, and from all accounts, Alex and Zach had managed to increase that fortune many times over. Even though she and her mom had always lived on her mom's meager earnings waiting tables at the local diner, Kat had never felt she'd truly suffered because they'd been poor. And even though her mom had always had very poor taste in men, Kat had grown up knowing her mother loved her unconditionally.

Kat had never felt money was all that important, and her mom had always emphasized the importance of a good education, the value in helping others, and always managed to fill their time together with love and laughter. Those were the lessons Kat had considered her mother's legacy, and those gifts had left little time for Kat to notice what they didn't have.

KAT HAD MET Jenna Lamont the very first day of first grade. Jenna had boldly walked up to the new girl in class despite Kat's attempts to disappear when she saw how much bigger all the other kids were and how nice they were all dressed. Jenna had stood in front of her and said, "I'm Jenna Lamont. You and I are going to be best friends."

Jenna had put her arm around Kat's shoulders and proceeded to walk her around the room, introducing her to each of their classmates. They'd been inseparable from that day forward. It had never mattered to Jenna that Kat's clothes came from the secondhand store; she had told Kat thousands of times, "It's what's inside a person that matters, the wrapping it comes in doesn't matter." Yes, Jenna Lamont had been a blessing in more ways than Kat could even begin to count.

Chapter 5

STEPPING INTO THE shower behind Katarina, Zach had to fight the urge to pull her into his arms, pin her against the wall, and plunge his cock deep in her sweet pussy and stay there for a week. Damn, she was gorgeous and even more petite than he'd remembered. She couldn't be over five foot one, and if she weighed more than a hundred pounds, he'd be shocked. Even though she was slender, she had delicious curves in all the right places, and he couldn't wait to run his tongue over every inch of her.

He planned to spend a lot of time finding every spot that would make her shiver and moan his name. Shaking his head, Zach tried to bring his wayward thoughts back to the present. Stepping in front of her just as Alex wrapped his arms around her from behind, Zach watched as Alex gave her a small taste of what it would be like when they bound her to their bed. Zach slowly ran his hands up her arms from her wrists to her shoulders and began kneading her stiff muscles, gently trying to coax them into releasing the tension they'd both noticed as soon as she'd known they would be joining her in the shower. Zach saw Alex's smile and knew they were both thinking the same thing… *Oh, Katarina, love, you are going to be naked and wet every chance we get.*

Kat's head fell back, and she groaned at Alex's hold and

Zach's touch. Zach could see her begin to relax as she leaned back against his brother's chest. He slid his hands down her chest to cup her breasts, just skimming the very surface of her skin and never touching her nipples. He dribbled scented body wash on to her chest and watched as Alex began washing her with slow, smooth circular motions.

Watching the bubbles slide down past her belly button and over her mound was enough to bring any man to his knees, and it was too much temptation for Zach to resist. Squatting down in front of Kat, he used a soft, well-soaped cloth to gently wash her legs, then massaged each foot, eliciting soft moans from her when he drew his thumbs the length of her arches.

"You like that, love?" Alex asked close to her ear. "We'll have to remember that, Zach. It seems our beautiful Katarina enjoys a foot massage. I wonder what else she might enjoy having rubbed." As he spoke, he pinched her nipples between his thumb and first finger and pulled gently, causing Kat to arch her back, pushing her breasts forward in invitation.

"Please…" was all Kat managed to say before reaching one hand back to wrap it around Alex's neck, pulling him tighter against her back. Zach watched her tense and knew the injuries to her back were more uncomfortable than she wanted them to know.

"Let's get your hair washed, and then we'll see what we can do to make sure you enjoy the rest of your shower, baby girl. Hold on to Zach while I work on your hair." Zach stood up, and Alex leaned Kat into his chest. Zach held her while Alex washed and conditioned her long hair. The silky strands turned the color of sun-ripened wheat and hung clear to her narrow waist when wet. Keeping her hair off her back as much as possible, Alex gently rinsed her abused back with the handheld water massager rather than allowing her to step under the shower's pulsing jets.

Alex pulled her gently back against his chest. At the same time, he placed his feet on the inside of hers and widened his stance, forcing her legs apart. When she tried to shift, he stilled her, whispering, "Let Zach make you feel good, love. Let him taste you. Just relax against me, and let us give you pleasure. We want to see what you look like when you come, sweetness." If he hadn't been holding her so close, he might have missed the subtle tightening of her muscles. "What's wrong? Talk to us, sweetheart."

Kat sighed and tried again to close her legs, but Zach had a firm hold of the inside of her thighs and his large hands easily held her legs apart.

"Well, um, you see, well, I haven't, well, I haven't ever, damn, this is so embarrassing. It's like this, I'm frigid. There it is, the sad truth that is Katarina McKay's life. I appreciate what you are trying to do, but I've never had an orgasm, and I know I'll just end up disappointing you." He watched her close her eyes, no doubt she was trying to block whatever reaction she feared. "Please, just let me go. I don't think I can deal with your pity or disgust right now. I just want to get out of the shower and find a hole to crawl into."

Zach squeezed her legs again, a bit more forcefully, and in a sharp voice said, "Kat, look at me... Now! If you've never had an orgasm, that's on your lover's shoulders, not yours. You are a passionate, very responsive woman. Let me show you how wonderful it can be when you let go of all that control and just feel."

"No, YOU DON'T understand, I know I can't compete with the other women you've made love to, and I'm not sure I'd survive knowing how much I'd let you down. Please, I just want to get out of the shower and get dressed." Kat was sure she'd turned about every shade of red known to exist. *God, I should have never come back to Climax. I'm never going to be able to show my face here again after this.*

"I swear, if you weren't already injured, I'd paddle your ass for spouting that nonsense. We're going to show you just how frigid you *aren't*, kitten," Zach said just before his mouth descended on her pussy. He proceeded to bring her to the very edge of her sanity twice before he slid his thick finger inside her.

Kat was sure she was losing her mind. She'd never felt like this. Every nerve ending in her entire body felt like it was beginning to vibrate and tingle at the same time. Holy hell, what Zach could do with his mouth. Alex had captured both of her wrists and was pinning them loosely behind her back while Zach was making love to her pussy with his mouth. Alex kept talking to her, his words alone could probably trigger orgasms in most women.

"Do you like the way Zach's tongue is circling your clit, Katarina? Can you imagine how good he's going to make you feel when he sucks it into his mouth? Do you like it when he pushes his fingers through your sweet juices and then presses them inside you with the perfect amount of pressure on the magic spot inside?" His voice was pure seduction, and Kat felt her knees begin to shake.

"His touch sends lightning through your entire body,

doesn't it, love? How many orgasms will it take for you to let go of your fear? Zach can keep you right on the edge for hours, you know, and then he'll send you over into oblivion whenever he chooses. How much pleasure can you take, Katarina? How much will be just enough? Or do you need a little bite of pain to send you soaring? Let's see what makes your beautiful body sing."

Alex pinched her nipples just as Zach pressed against her G-spot, and Kat's world exploded in showers of brilliant light and electric shocks which had her screaming their names as her knees buckled. Her pussy flooded, and she was sure the heated tingling sensation racing over her skin was never going to end. They brought her down slowly, her body shuddering as she felt the tide within her ebb slowly away.

ZACH LEANED BACK on his heels, smiling. "She is so beautiful when she comes, and she tastes like the sweetest peach I've ever eaten. I can't wait for you to see the rapture on Kat's face when her orgasm overtakes her, brother." Katarina McKay was everything they'd always known she'd be... stunning in her responsiveness and a natural submissive.

Zach knew Alex had used his hold on her wrists as a simple way to test her response to bondage and control, and she'd tumbled head first into a submissive mind-set, almost instinctively. Both he and his brother knew often something as simple as restraining a sub's hands in your own was enough to trigger a response in a true submissive, and Kat had responded perfectly. He planned to spend the rest of his life learning every nuance that made Kat who she was, and he was going to enjoy every second of the exploration.

Chapter 6

KAT COULDN'T BELIEVE the way her body still vibrated with residual pleasure. Holy hell, no wonder people were always talking about the 'Big O.' If she'd known it would be like *that,* she wouldn't still be a virgin that's for sure. Damn and double damn, that was a whole other problem, she didn't even want to think about how they might respond to that little news flash. Maybe if she managed to get out of here really soon, they'd never have to know. *Yeah, right. They won't even let you pee in peace, and you think you are going to get away from them long enough to get out of the building? Not fracking likely!*

After they'd gently patted her dry with a towel big enough to wrap them all in, they'd left her in the bedroom while they went to their rooms to get dressed, promising they'd bring her something to wear when they returned. So, here she sat on the window seat, looking out over the paradise they'd created behind the mansion. Kat enjoyed watching as the tiny lights swayed in the breeze, making it look like the whole garden was alive with a million dancing fireflies.

She'd only gotten a brief glimpse of her surroundings earlier and couldn't wait to explore things more fully. Of course, her lack of clothing was going to be a serious problem and one she couldn't see either Alex or Zach being too anxious to help her solve. If she could just get in touch with Jenna, she was sure her friend would help her go into town for a bit of shopping. She'd need to get to her computer or her cell phone soon. Maybe they'd take her to her car or better yet, have it moved up to the house for her. With her car close, she'd be able to leave as soon as she got the stitches out and figured out a safe place to go. Jenna would help her find a new location. Kat just needed to be able to contact her best friend without spilling the beans about the trouble she was in.

ALEX STOOD IN the doorway, watching Katarina look out the window. He could always tell when her mind was working at warp speed because she chewed on her bottom lip and talked to herself.

"It's not going to happen, you know." She spun around so quickly he saw her wince before she was able to mask it. "Jenna isn't going to come and spirit you away. For one thing, she'd know we'd be watching for her and for another, she is avoiding this place like the plague because of Colt."

"Colt?"

"Colt Matthews is our chief of security. He was our team leader and has been our friend for more years than I care to think about. He and Jenna have a mutual attraction they are both fighting. Instead of seeing where it might lead, they pick at each other like a couple of kindergarteners. We've been amused by it, but we're probably going to have to give them a little shove soon. Their verbal sparring is starting to be a distraction and it's damned annoying for everyone around them."

Alex pushed away from the door and moved into the room. He walked to Kat, taking her hand in his and pulling her to her feet. "Raise your arms up, Katarina, I have something for you to wear so you won't be chilled when we go downstairs for dinner. There are often others eating at this time—employees, friends, Club members we want you to meet—but we'd rather you were dressed… for now."

Alex's sly smile told her he didn't plan to always have her dressed in front of his friends. Why didn't that make her angry? She didn't understand her reactions to either Alex or Zach. Even though the idea of being naked in front of their club members scared her, it was also exciting. God, maybe her college boyfriend had been right… maybe she was sick and twisted.

"Christ, what I wouldn't give to know what just went through that sharp little mind of yours." Zach had been standing behind Alex, watching the play of emotions move across her face. It was obvious she'd responded positively to Alex's not-so-subtle reference to having her naked in front of others in the future, but then he'd seen what had looked too much like shame in her eyes. That was definitely something they would need to explore, there would be no place for shame in their relationship.

Kat raised her hands and felt Zach move behind her, placing his hands on her hips, and sliding his hands up in a slow, seductive move that had goose bumps breaking out all over her body. Alex dropped the silk chemise over her head and let it slide down her body. The dress was a beautiful midnight blue and fit her perfectly. It fell to just a few inches above her knees and flared slightly from the waist, so it would swish when she walked. God, she loved clothes that swished.

"Beautiful," was all Alex said as he lifted her hair and spread it over her shoulders. "Let's go. I'm sure you must be starving."

"Hold on, I'm not ready yet. I don't have any panties or shoes." Kat stood with her hands on her hips, looking at the two of them like they'd lost their minds.

"You don't need panties. We'd just rip them off you, so what's the point? Hell, if we have our way, you'll never wear the damned things again." Zach was obviously trying to not grin at the wide-eyed look she was sure had been on her face before it flushed wildly. "And we don't allow subs to wear shoes in The Club unless they are of the 'fuck me' variety, so having you barefoot won't be seen as unusual to anyone you might meet at dinner."

"Seriously? You want me to eat dinner without panties? That's just... Well, it's just wrong! I can't go down there with just this dress covering me. What if someone knows I'm not wearing underwear? God, they'll think I'm a—" She was cut off by Alex.

"They'll think you are a gorgeous woman, and they'll be jealous as hell of the two of us. Now come on, it's time to eat." He grabbed her hand and had her halfway down the hall before she even realized they'd moved.

Frick fracking fudge. Her mother had always told her to choose her battles, and she was pretty sure this wasn't the time to argue. Likely, there would be other issues more worthy of the effort it would take to argue, and to be honest, she was indeed starving. Giving herself a pep talk, she vowed to be stronger and take control back from them as soon as she'd gotten some dinner. That's right, she just needed fuel... *Right, and you can watch for the sun to rise in the west tomorrow, too.*

AS THEY WALKED toward the dining room, they could hear loud voices laughing and joking, the boisterous sounds of people who knew each other well. They were enjoying themselves, laughing and teasing one another in the way longtime friends do. The minute Alex and Zach led Kat into the room, everyone fell silent. Kat had been standing between Alex and Zach, but quickly took a step back and tried to step behind Zach before Alex tightened his hold on her hand and drew her back between them.

"Everyone, I'd like you to meet Katarina. Katarina, we'll introduce you to everyone after we're all seated." Alex's unspoken order was clear, and everyone began moving to their seats around the biggest table Kat had ever seen in a private residence. Holy shit, it must seat at least thirty people.

Kat sat between Alex and Zach, listening as they introduced her to employees and friends, resigned to the knowledge she wasn't going to remember even a fraction of that they were telling her because as soon as she'd settled in her seat, they'd each put a hand on the knee closest to them and pulled her legs apart. While Alex was making the introductions, Zach had leaned close and whispered, "When you sit with us, this is how we'll want you. Accessible." When Kat tried to slowly move her legs back together, they had each tightened their hold on her thighs, and at Zach's low growl, she stilled once again.

She hoped there wouldn't be a quiz later about all the introductions, job titles, hometowns, or general information they were throwing at her. She was sure her eyes were beginning to glaze over as their hands began gentle massaging strokes, bringing them both closer and closer to her now soaking wet pussy. From the knowing looks she was getting from most of the others at the table, she was sure everyone knew what the rats were doing to her. God, could she be any more embarrassed?

I can do this, just concentrate on something benign, jigsaw puzzles, yeah, that's nice and boring. I'll just think about—okay, what was I going to think about... Oh God, that feels so good... Oh yeah, just a little more to the center and I'll be able to... Oh Shit, I can't do this here! Kat straightened up in her chair; the scalding looks she sent each of them was met with matching wicked, knowing grins. *Damn them both. They know exactly what they're doing to me.*

Alex leaned toward her and said, "Don't worry Katarina, we won't make you come in front of others... yet. For now, those sounds are for our ears only. You aren't yet ready for that, we'll know when you are, baby, trust us to know what you need."

Kat knew her heart wouldn't survive their rejection a second time. She was convinced Alex and Zach were looking for a woman well versed in the ways of passion as well as their chosen lifestyle. It was only a matter of time until they found out she wasn't as experienced as they seemed to think she was and she didn't doubt for a minute rejection would be a certainty.

Learning about the Lamonts' lifestyle had taught Kat she had misinterpreted the scene she'd walked in on years ago as abuse. But she'd also learned true Dominants placed a lot of value on experience and compliance, two traits she was certain the good Lord had failed to give her in any measure. There just wasn't any way to make this work; she needed to get her head back on straight and figure out a way to move on as soon as possible. But first, she'd have to find out exactly what measures they'd taken to ensure her safety because anything which had been put in place to keep others out would also keep her closed in.

Chapter 7

K AT MANAGED TO deflect questions throughout dinner not only from Alex and Zach, but also their Chief Snoop as she'd quickly nicknamed Colt Matthews. Cripes, the man was a kick-ass interrogator in a designer package. He was taller than Alex and Zach, and his six-foot four-inch frame was broader. He reminded her of a very large refrigerator with monster feet and an even bigger attitude. She suspected his apparent disdain toward her had more to do with her friendship with Jenna than it had to do with her, but that didn't make dealing with him any more pleasant. If he thought being a jerk was the way to get information from her, he was about as insightful as a refrigerator also.

After dinner, Alex took her hand and led her to his office. Zach, Colt, and several other members of their security team also moved into the room. There was also a much older man off to the side, she couldn't remember his name, but she was fairly sure they'd mentioned he was not only a friend but also their attorney.

Looking around the room, Kat was impressed with the feel of casual elegance in the décor. When it had been their father's office, it had been much more formal, but the soft leather furnishings and beautiful wildlife prints had softened the room's appearance. It was obvious the office was used for a variety of purposes because there was a long conference table at one end as well as a grouping of chairs facing a massive stone fireplace at the other end. Since the office was in the back corner of the house, two walls were entirely made of floor-to-ceiling glass. Kat knew the view would overlook the main entrance leading to the house and The Club as well as giving them a partial view of the back gardens and pool area. *Gonna be pretty difficult to fly under their damned radar in this place; welcome to Sing Sing West.*

Positioning her between them, Alex and Zach sat on the smaller of the sofas. Alex turned toward her. "Katarina, we need you to tell us who we're dealing with and what we're up against." Boy, directly to the point as always.

Suddenly a picture from an old movie she'd watched as a kid flashed through her mind; she felt like the suspect sitting on a stool in a dark room with a light pointed directly at her face. She would be blinded while being questioned by the menacing shadowy figure pacing behind the light. It might have just been a split second of distraction, but she still fought the urge to shudder at the image. It was a little too much like the scene that had gotten her into this damned mess. Her, bathed in a brilliant spotlight surrounded by darkness, with someone asking questions. Damn. Okay, so the whip was different, and oh yeah, the guy in the movie wasn't wearing leathers, but... suddenly Kat realized she'd taken a leisurely mental side trip. *Uh oh.*

"Katarina?" Alex wondered where on earth she'd gone. He knew she had heard the question, but then it was if she'd just completely blanked out for several seconds. PTSD? Definitely something he'd want to discuss with his brother and Colt.

Glancing around the room at all the eyes trained on

her, Kat took a deep breath and began. She started by explaining how she'd started her own web-design business, so she could stay under the radar, so to speak. One of her first clients had been Cal-Corp Industries. At their wide-eyed expression, she conceded she'd been ignorant of the rumors about the company's true sources of revenue. All she'd known was they'd been willing to pay her huge sums of money to design and maintain various web pages for different branches of their business.

Working with them had been easy at first; they'd only met via webcam, and all payments had been made by direct deposit. They'd always sent information to her either electronically or by messenger, so she hadn't had any personal contact with anyone from the company for almost the first four years of her contract. But during the last year, things had gotten much more complicated.

Thinking back over the years she'd done work for Cal-Corp, Kat was again amazed at how easily she'd been led right in to the middle of a nightmare she still couldn't completely wrap her mind around. She tried to explain how it had started when they requested she design a site to deal with young women wanting to *study abroad*. The site was supposed to tell prospective women about opportunities to "earn free room and board" in return for "simple household or nanny duties." They'd added little changes along the way that together would have thrown up huge red flags, but when they'd been brought forth so subtly several weeks and months apart, they'd failed to alert her to the true purpose of the site.

Colt was the first to interrupt her. "So, it never occurred to you they might be running a sex slave trafficking business via the web page you'd designed and were maintaining?" His disbelief was obvious from the tone of his voice, and she bristled at the accusation.

"Well, no, I guess I was naïve, but when you aren't a criminal yourself, you don't always know how they think." She glared back at him and didn't care if he thought she was accusing him of being less than a stellar citizen because he'd seen it so quickly. She didn't need to justify herself to him, and the sooner he decided she wasn't worth the effort, the sooner he'd ignore her long enough for her to slip past him and his merry band of prison guards.

Colt returned her glare as she continued to explain in as much detail as she could remember how she'd come to start talking to Cal Robertson, the son of electronics mogul Calvin Robertson, Sr. She hesitantly added that they had long chats about everything, and she'd considered Cal a friend. When she had confided her interest in BDSM during one of their many late-night chats, he'd told her he'd be happy to answer all her questions as he had a lot of experience in the lifestyle.

God, could this be any more humiliating? Here she sat, telling all these men how she'd chatted up a virtual stranger about her interest in all things kinky. And two of the men were ones she'd been in love with since she'd been a junior high school girl with stars in her eyes, adoring her best friend's older brothers from afar. While they'd always been polite, they'd never really seemed to take much notice of her. They'd been six years older than she and Jenna, so seeing them when they'd been home from college had always been the highlight of her summer and Christmas breaks. Even though a part of her wanted to just sit back and drift through her memories of those happier times in her life, she shifted in her seat and continued.

By the time Kat had explained everything—well, almost everything—about how she'd come to be at the

BDSM club in Las Vegas where Cal had decided to show her how refusing him would be dealt with, she was beyond exhausted. Leaning her head against Zach's shoulder, she let her eyes close slowly. Somewhere in the back of her mind, she heard Alex speak.

"Gentlemen, I believe Katarina needs to rest now. You have enough information to begin your investigation. Since you've retrieved her computer from her car, please begin there. We need to gather everything we can to nail this son of a bitch." Then, turning to Colt, he spoke quietly, "Call this in, make sure you let the brass know we're working on this thing. I know we don't do domestic, but the ring is international, so they can't balk too much. Let them know it's nonnegotiable, and we'll turn over everything we come up with."

Zach slid his arms under Kat's knees and lifted her into his arms. He started toward her suite as Alex finished up the meeting and saw everyone out. She felt safe and cuddled up against him, inhaling the clean scent of his soap. She hoped they didn't know how much of the story she'd edited for their benefit or simply omitted. There were lots of ways to get at the truth, and she was certain he and Alex would find something that not only be effective, but would lead to their mutual enjoyment also.

Chapter 8

KAT CAME AWAKE when she heard a moan and slowly figured out it was her own. She quickly realized why her body felt like it was tingling all over. Her legs were spread wide open and being held in place by something wrapped around her ankles. Her hands were bound with her palms facing one another and secured above her head.

Opening her eyes slowly, Kat saw candle light dancing on the ceiling, tiny points of light reflected from candles sitting on every available flat surface. Looking to each side, she saw Alex and Zach lying on their sides, propped up on their elbows, watching her intently. They were slowly drawing the backs of their fingers up and down her body, leaving goose bumps in their wake.

Alex was the first to speak. "We'd like to talk to you, baby. We have the feeling there might be things you forgot to mention when we spoke to you downstairs." Uh oh, this didn't seem like it was going to be a regular, get-together-over-coffee-and-chitchat session to her.

"You didn't leave out anything did you, kitten?" Zach's voice was soft, but there was an edge to it she couldn't explain, but Kat didn't want to focus too much on that right at this moment. How did they expect her to think clearly when they had her tied down and they were lighting her up with warm sensations? Somewhere in the back of her mind, she'd known her smoke-and-mirrors version wouldn't get her by forever, but she hadn't expected this. *This* was going to be a whole new method of interrogation, she was sure of that much.

"Well, of course, I didn't recount each and every moment of the last seven years. That would have taken hours. I told you everything you need to know to protect yourselves until I am well enough to travel. Honestly, I don't think there's anything to worry about. I was always careful to avoid telling anyone where I was from. There isn't any way Cal will be able to find me here before I move on. I'm sorry if you feel I've brought trouble to your doorstep. If you'll just help me get my car from the woods, I think I'll be able to travel in the next day or so." She tried to sound upbeat even when she didn't know exactly where she'd go. She was out of cash and was certain any attempt to access her bank accounts would lead Cal straight to her.

"Your car is locked up securely in one the sheds down by the garage. Anything you needed from it has been brought up to the house." Alex's calmly spoken words didn't match the tension that seemed to be coursing through him. Not a good sign at all.

ALEX WAS PISSED—PLAIN and simple. Completely irate. His little sister had a lot of explaining to do, and when she returned to Climax later this week, they'd be waiting. Colt's team had found Katarina's computer in her car and accessed her personal e-mail only to discover their darling sister had known where Katarina was and had been communicating with her best friend for years. While Jenna might not have known in the beginning where Katarina was, she had certainly known for a good long time, and it seemed she'd not seen fit to share that information with her older brothers. Zach was equally pissed, and he was usually Jenna's biggest ally.

Slowly drawing their fingers up and around Katarina's sensitive breasts, they let the silence grow until she was starting to twist and pull at her restraints.

"Hold still or you'll hurt yourself. We aren't going to hurt you, we just want to ask you about a few things and play a bit at the same time. You see, one of the wonderful things about you being so responsive is that your body will betray you if you try to lie to us. It will be like having you attached to a lie detector, only a lot more fun, don't you think?" Kat knew Alex prided himself on being intimidating and always in control of a situation, but holy shit, this icy version of Alex was downright frightening.

At the mention of a lie detector, Kat had tensed; if she'd been covered, they might have missed it. Oh, yes, Alex loved this method of information retrieval. Smiling at his brother, he knew Zach wouldn't have missed the small tell either.

"Now, Katarina, tell me, when is the last time you had any communication with Jenna."

"Oh, well, gee... let me think... it's been—" Kat's words were cut short when Alex squeezed her nipple sharply, causing her to suck in her breath and freeze.

"Let me remind you, love, we've gained possession of your car and have retrieved its contents. Let me *also* remind you we have a security team highly trained in a wide variety of helpful skills, including computer hacking. Now, I'll ask you again, when is the last time you had any contact with Jenna?"

Oh shit, this was going to be really bad. Jenna had been e-mailing and Skyping with her for several years. They had no doubt seen her last e-mail to Jenna, detailing how scared she was about Cal's increasing obsession with her. Hard to tell at this point which one of them was in the most trouble, but if she was placing bets, she'd lay money on Jenna… But truthfully, it could go either way.

"Okay, we've been talking for a while. I asked her to not mention it to you because I knew you didn't want me, and it just seemed like it would be less heartache for everybody if you didn't feel like you were obligated to look out for me. I didn't think I'd be able to listen to the 'you're just like a sister to us' speech again. And Jenna reluctantly, *very reluctantly*, agreed to keep my confidence."

"I promise you, we'll deal with Mata Hari Jenna when she returns home later this week. I'm tempted to let Colt deal with her; he's been itching to paddle her ass for years." When Kat started to speak, he placed his finger over her lips and continued, "No, you know that lying by omission is still lying and so does she. We'll deal with her later. Now, let's talk about all the points of your story that didn't seem to make it in to the Reader's Digest version you gave us earlier this evening, including Cal Robertson's obsession with you."

Alex smiled to himself when he saw Zach's hand make its way to her pussy. The scent of her arousal filled the air, so there wasn't much chance his brother would miss how wet this whole interrogation and bondage scene was making their little reluctant sub.

Kat tossed her head from one side to the other in search of an escape. "Damn and double damn, how do I always find myself in the worst positions with men?" He knew she hadn't intended to mutter the words aloud. Far be it from him to spoil what may well be their best method of information gathering.

As always, lots of sexual tension and foreplay, but never any of the good stuff. Shit, at this rate she was going to be the only virgin in the local nursing home. Kat was going to go insane if Zach didn't stop playing with her pussy. She didn't have a prayer of hiding her arousal from them.

"Well, I maybe glossed over how interested Cal is in me. Obsession really is a very strong word, but he—" Kat's words were cut off again when Zach pulled the hood back from her clit and leaned down to blow on it, sending what felt like electric shocks out from her core. "Holy shit! How am I supposed to think when you do that?"

"You might want to think about just telling the truth. Give us the facts we need, and we'll give you what you need in return. Remember, good behavior is rewarded, and bad behavior is punished; it really is just that simple, Katarina." Alex's words were softly spoken, but the edge of steel was obvious. Kat knew he was tired of her dancing around the subject, but he wasn't going to like the truth either.

Knowing she'd better come clean, she told them about how Cal had taken her phone and provided her with a *better model*. Now, she might be young, but she'd made a living working with computer technology long enough to know she'd been given a phone enabling Cal and his merry band of crazies to track her every move. Before she'd left Las Vegas, she'd disabled the tracking, hoping she'd have at least a few days' head start.

The more she explained, the more intimate their touches became until she was all but panting with desire. "Please, I can't take any more. Either fuck me or leave me alone. You're torturing me and you both know it."

At this point, Kat didn't care if they got mad and left the bed, she'd taken matters in to her own hands for years, and she'd take care of the need slamming into her now if they didn't want to.

"Now, let's discuss your sexual experience, kitten." Zach had moved down so his shoulders were holding her legs even further apart and his face was right between her legs. She could feel his breath on her spread pussy lips, and she knew he had a front row seat to her arousal. "When had you planned to tell us you are still a virgin? Hmmm? That's really a pretty important piece of information seeing as how you are asking us to fuck you. Don't you think?"

Oh God, every time she thought she couldn't be more embarrassed, she was proven wrong. Knowing her face was glowing a nice bright red, Kat closed her eyes, trying to block out her humiliation.

"OPEN YOUR EYES. Now, kitten. You'll not hide from us. We won't allow it, ever." Zach knew she'd be embarrassed, but they weren't going to let her get away with hiding anything from them. He and Alex both believed the old adage, *you should always begin as you intend to go*, so they might as well convince her now there wasn't anything about her they didn't intend to know.

There was no room in any D/s relationship for deception. Without a solid foundation, no relationship could survive, and one involving not only their lifestyle, but adding in the fact it would be a ménage was going to require an even greater level of communication and trust. Kat was about to get her first lesson in all the ways they could bring her pleasure, the likes of which she'd never experienced, as well as the creative ways they could punish her.

"The fact you are a virgin means you'll be giving us the greatest of gifts, Kat. It also means that we need to take particular care that you're really ready to take our cocks. That's enough talking for now. We want to play with you for a while. But know this, you can stop thinking about leaving us. We won't lose you again, kitten. You belong to us, both of us, and the sooner you figure that out, the better we'll all get along."

Alex kept his tone low and deep, marveling at the way her body responded so perfectly. "There are rules you'll need to follow, but since it's obvious you have been doing your homework on our lifestyle, we'll assume you are well-versed in at least the basics of the Dom-sub dynamic. We are neither one interested in owning a slave. We'll expect you to submit fully to us both in all things sexual whether they are taking place in the bedroom or any other place of our choosing. But outside of that, we'll respect you as the strong, independent, capable woman we know you are, and we'll demand your respect in return. The only time our instructions outside of the bedroom will be nonnegotiable is when they relate to your safety."

Zach had been running his fingers from her clit all the way back to her puckered rosette and then reversing the path while Alex had been speaking to her. They wanted her to associate the rules with her pleasure. They also hoped it would temper her reaction to the restrictions they'd be imposing on her.

Kat's eyes glazed over in a lust-filled haze and Alex knew Zach was keeping her as close to the edge as he dared. Until they had a chance to learn every nuance of her responses, they'd have to be careful to not bring her to completion until they intended to. Judging by the personal massager they'd found in her small overnight case, she hadn't been shy about providing for her own pleasure. They planned to explain, very clearly, that her pleasure now belonged exclusively to them.

Chapter 9

A S ZACH MOVED to release her leg restraints, Alex freed her hands and massaged her shoulders. Kissing each of her finger tips, he said, "It will always be our greatest pleasure to provide you with everything you need, Katarina, don't ever forget that—even when we may not agree on what is best for you. Keep in mind what you *need* may not always be what you *want;* you'll need to learn to trust us to know the difference. We aren't going to fuck you tonight."

Kat struggled to sit up only to be held firmly in place by both men.

"Now, see, this is where trust is so very important. I said we weren't going to fuck you, we don't want your first time to be like that. We are both going to make love to you, but not until you are truly ready for us. Now let's see what we can do about helping with this virginity issue which seems to be weighing so heavily on your mind."

Alex captured her mouth with his and began to kiss her in a way that could only be described as pure oral seduction. His tongue slowly traced the seam of her lips until she opened to him with a soft moan he felt in the deepest levels of his very soul. She was his, she belonged between him and his brother. If it took him the rest of his life, he would gladly spend it showing her all the ways they could prove their devotion to her. He'd lost his heart to her when he'd returned from college one Christmas, and Alex knew Zach had loved her as long if not longer.

Zach had been right when he'd said it hadn't been the right time. But now? Now the time was perfect. They planned to use every skill—both physical and emotional—they'd ever learned as Doms to make sure she never called another place home. She was theirs, it was just that simple.

ZACH WATCHED HIS brother kiss Kat and was awed by how right it felt. There was no jealousy, just pure pleasure at seeing Alex and Kat begin what he knew was going to be a life-changing evening for all three of them. Zach moved his fingers back and forth along the swollen folds of Kat's pussy, causing a fresh rush of her sweet nectar to coat his fingers. Slowly, he slid his middle finger inside her.

"Kitten, you are so tight, we're going to have to stretch you a bit first. We don't want to hurt you any more than necessary. There will be a bit of pain, but you already know that, don't you?" When she nodded, he added, "We'll make sure that small bit of pain is worth it, I promise."

Curving his finger forward, Zach pressed a few strokes over the spongy area he knew would increase her arousal exponentially and marveled at the way she canted her hips forward, pressing closer to his touch. She was so wonderfully responsive. Her skin was beginning to flush, and he wondered what shade of pink her ass would turn the first time she was turned over his knee for a spanking. Her injuries were healing nicely, and it was going to be a privilege to show her the joys of erotic spankings when her body was fully recovered. But for now, he'd concentrate on making her first experience of sexual intercourse as pleasurable as possible.

WHEN ZACH SLID a second finger inside her, Kat thought she was going to come right then. If his fingers felt this amazing, how was she ever going to survive their cocks? From the looks of the bulges she'd noticed earlier this evening, they might not even fit inside her.

"Don't worry, baby," Alex whispered as if sensing her question, "we'll make sure you are ready for us. You may not think we'll fit, but I assure you, we will. It's going to be amazing, you'll see. Just lay back and feel. Let your mind float in the pleasure. Let yourself fall headlong into the experience."

Katarina's mind was racing, tortured thoughts about how disappointed they'd be kept rearing their ugly heads. She knew Alex and Zach well enough to be sure they'd already discussed every detail of their time with her.

"We're going to make this moment magical for you, kitten. We want you to remember this night forever. It'll be one of our fondest memories when we're all old and gray, rocking on the front porch, watching our grandchildren play in the yard."

"Baby, are you on birth control?" Alex wanted to make sure she knew they would protect her in all ways. "We both have current doctor's reports and can show you we're clean. We have never had sex without a condom. But you are ours and we'd both like to feel you without anything between us if possible."

Kat was almost panting with desire. "I'm on the pill. I have been for years." Kat felt them both freeze, so she added, "The doctor said it would regulate my monthly cycle and ease cramping. I continued taking them for that reason." She could practically feel their relief; it had always amazed her men thought if a single woman was taking birth control pills, it was because she wanted to be fucking like a bunny. For some reason, it didn't seem to occur to them there might be a legitimate medical reason involved.

Zach had moved up so his knees moved her legs farther apart as he slowly lowered himself over her and captured her mouth with his. The kiss ramped up her desire until she was almost unconsciously spreading her legs even farther apart and lifting her hips up in need. She felt him place the head of his cock at her opening and move inside just enough for her to feel the swollen tissues beginning to stretch around his width.

ZACH WAS FIGHTING the urge to plunge as deep as he could get into Kat's silky, wet heat. Hell, he was already digging deep for every bit of self-control he could muster, and he'd only just started making love to her. The combination of feeling her bare flesh surrounding his bare cock, along with his knowledge he was finally getting to make love to the woman he'd loved for so long, was almost more than he could comprehend.

Kat looked up at him, her hair spread across her pillow in soft, blonde waves of silk. Her eyes were filled with wonder and lust, her breathing becoming increasingly shallower, and he knew her pulse was racing. He began to slowly move in and out of her, gaining entrance in fractions of an inch with each stroke, trying to make sure her body had plenty of time to adjust. Both he and his brother were large men, and she was a very small woman; extra care was more important than his own need to plunder and stake his claim.

Zach felt the head of his cock come up against the membrane barrier of her innocence. He stilled and spoke against her ear. "This is it, kitten, I'm going to push through. It's going to sting, and I don't want you to feel like you need to hide your discomfort from us. We want all of you, remember that always. Hang onto my shoulders."

Before she had a chance to process everything he said and tense up, he was through. Zach heard her gasp and knew before he lifted his face back up to hers there would be tears running past her temples. He kissed them away.

"I'm sorry for your pain, but I will be forever grateful for the gift you have just given us. Your innocence is the most precious gift either of us has ever received, we'll treasure it always. You are truly ours, your body has not known another man, you are ours alone, and that's something we'll honor for the rest of our lives."

"You feel so amazing, I can't even begin to tell you how wonderful it is to feel you wrapping my cock in your wet heat. You feel like wet velvet, and my sweet kitten, the muscles of your pussy are already beginning to flutter around me. Ahh, Alex, you aren't going to believe how wonderful she feels. Her pussy started rippling around me from the first moment I made it inside her." Zach knew even though Alex had moved aside to allow the moment to be as intimate between them as possible, it was important Kat always thought of them as equal partners to her.

KAT WAS SURPRISED at how her body seemed to be making room for Zach. She'd been momentarily stunned by the sharp pain that had come when he pushed through her virginity, and she was so grateful he hadn't seemed to mind her tears. She'd never forget how special he'd made her feel and how he'd taken so much time to make sure she was really ready to take this step with them. As he began to move back and forth inside her, she felt as if a spring was being wound up tight inside of her and wondered how it was going to feel when he finally pushed her over the edge of pleasure.

True to his word, he really was making love to her. Even though she hadn't experienced it before, she was certain this was much different from the "fucking" she'd asked for, and she was also certain it wasn't at all how they usually dealt with their past submissives. As if knowing her thoughts were straying, Zach began to move faster, and he changed the angle ever so slightly, bringing her attention sharply back to the moment.

"Stay right here, kitten. I want you with me. I don't know where you went, but you need to be right here. Let me see what I can do to make sure I keep your undivided attention, hmmm?" And with that, he began long, fast strokes that brought her higher each time the tip of his cock pressed against her womb.

Kat was blindsided by the orgasm that washed over her; it swept every conscious thought out of her mind as it sent her spinning into an abyss of brilliant lights and color. She barely registered Zach's shout of completion as she felt his cock jerk and pulse, his seed filling her. Her arms fell to the side, and she was sure her muscles had all turned to mush. Zach held her tight against his chest as his breathing began to slowly return to normal.

When Kat was finally able to speak, her voice was filled with excitement and awe. "Oh my God. That was the most amazing thing I've ever experienced. I can't believe how wonderful that feels. No wonder everybody is always raving about sex. Who knew? Damn!"

Kat was rambling, she knew it, but try as she might, she just couldn't stop the words from tumbling out. "I really want to do that again, but I'm not sure I'll be able to move for a while. Is it always like that? Why didn't I know about this?" Again, with the rambling, geez, she really needed to get a grip on her mouth.

ALEX HAD WATCHED his brother make sweet love to Katarina, and it was without a doubt the single most moving experience of his life. It was also hottest thing he'd ever seen, and considering the fact they owned a successful BDSM club, that was saying a lot. But her reaction, her giddy babbling, was a completely joyful surprise. She was overwhelmed with happiness, and the utter bliss in her expression was truly something to behold. He found himself chuckling, something he'd have never thought he'd do in the bedroom. Life with Katarina would never be dull that was for certain.

AS ZACH PULLED himself from her body, he sat back and watched his seed seep from her depths. There was something on the most basic, primal level that was very satisfying about seeing his mark between her thighs. There were also streaks of blood; he used the warm, wet washcloth Alex handed him to gently remove the evidence of her lost virginity, so it wouldn't alarm her if she looked down. She'd tried to take the rag from his hand, but he'd stilled her and explained it was his duty and pleasure to care for her. She would become accustomed to their pampering in time, and they had all the time in the world to show her how cherished she would always be.

Chapter 10

KAT WATCHED ALEX move in along her side as Zach moved away. Her heart rate was slowly returning to normal, and she was starting to regain control of her mouth, or perhaps it was just running out of steam. It had always been the bane of her existence. Her inability to control her jabbering often got her in to all sorts of trouble; when she was nervous, stuff just tumbled out and usually in a jumbled-up mess. But for right now, she was just enjoying the floating feeling Zach had left her with. It was no small wonder why people loved sex, no siree. She'd never really understood its appeal before, but it was crystal clear now... *Wow*!

Turning her face toward Alex, she was struck by the look of pure lust in his expression. His eyes were so dark, there didn't seem to be any color in them at all, and he was focused on her with such intent it was almost palpable. Brushing her hand softly down the side of his face, she watched his eyes become even more passion filled, as his nostrils flared. Alex leaned forward, brushing his lips softly over hers.

"Watching you and my brother make love was the most arousing thing I have ever seen. Knowing you saved yourself for us humbles me; I want you to know how cherished that gift is. We'll hold it close to our hearts forever, never doubt that, love.

"You are glowing, you know that? Making love suits you, seeing your face as you fall over the edge into the bliss of your pleasure is beautiful beyond words. But remember, we won't always make love to you, there will be times when we will fuck you, and there will be times when it won't be about your pleasure, only ours. But tonight? Baby, tonight is all about making sure you know the pleasure we can bring you. Tonight, we'll both worship your body and take joy in knowing we've shown you how precious you are."

Kat knew the Lamonts well enough to hear what Alex *hadn't* said. They would make sure tonight was about making her fall in love with them, but what happened when they grew tired of her? Her heart wouldn't survive their rejection a second time. It didn't surprise Kat that Alex could make love with his words as well as his body. Kat had always known just because they were twins didn't mean they were the same person. It had always amazed Kat that some people didn't even bother to find out which brother they were dealing with and even fewer took the time to get to know them as individuals.

She'd always been able to tell them apart and had agreed with Jenna in her confusion about why others found it so difficult. Sure, they looked a lot alike, but there were subtle differences she'd always seen. Jenna had always insisted their personality differences alone were enough to make their physical appearances differ. While they both still carried themselves with a distinctly military posture, Alex had always seemed more formidable, his gaze penetrating straight to the depths of your soul.

Zach was more approachable; it seemed like they had perfected the good-cop-bad-cop routine long before they would have known what it meant. Even from a distance, it was obvious their goals were the same, but the means to that end would always be different. Oh, how she wished with everything in her she could stay, that she could be the woman to fulfill the role of wife and mother of their children, but it just couldn't be.

"What's swirling around inside that sharp mind of yours, Katarina? Your eyes are shining, and I know your thoughts are moving at the speed of light."

Kat continued to caress the side of Alex's face. "I was thinking how different you and Zach are in some ways, yet so similar in others. Being an only child, I loved having siblings vicariously through Jenna when we were in grammar school. Growing up in Climax was a blessing in so many ways; I learned that relationships don't have to look like what our culture dictates in order to be successful. I also learned being true to oneself is more important than following rules defined by others." Then giggling, she added, "And by spying on the Lamont twins, I learned a lot about sex."

"Is that so? Well, let's see just how much of that illicitly gained knowledge you remember. Perhaps you'd like to demonstrate some of that skill? We're going to have a serious conversation about D/s relationships, hard and soft limits negotiations, and safe words, but not tonight. *Tonight* is about making sure you know the joys of making love. We want you to always remember this night."

Alex knew forging a bond with Katarina had to be their number one priority if they were to rebuild her fragile trust—trust that had been shattered first by the two of them and then more recently by Calvin Robertson. That asshole had put himself squarely on their radar. Soon they would know more about him than even his closest confidants knew, and then they'd use their considerable connections to bring everything down around him.

ALEX SLOWLY LOWERED his lips to hers and kissed her with such sweetness, it stole Kat's breath. The man kissed with his soul, reeling her in until she forgot anything existed aside from the man holding her. Kat had never really thought kissing was all it was cracked up to be, but Alex and Zach seemed to have elevated kissing to an art form. She soon found herself lost in the sensation of his lips pressed firmly against hers, his tongue doing a slow exploration of her mouth.

"I could kiss you forever," he whispered when he finally pulled back, "you are so very sweet. But I need to be inside you. I need to feel your warm pussy wrapped around me, squeezing my cock, your muscles trying to pull me back inside when I pull from your depths. I need to make love to you, baby. I want you to turn over and get up onto your hands and knees."

At her startled expression, he smiled. "I think your back has had enough friction from the bedding, and I want you to experience something a little different this time." When she moved into position, he continued, "There you go, let's put these pillows under you to help you stay in place. Now lower your head and shoulders down on to the bed and spread those beautiful legs apart for me."

Kat hesitated, biting her lip, and looking back over her shoulder at Alex.

"Katarina, remember, in the future any hesitance will be punished. Now be a good girl and get into position. I want you to feel everything I have to give you, and I want to enjoy this without worrying I'm putting more pressure on your injuries. They are healing nicely, and I don't want to do anything that will re-open those wounds."

Turning, she eased herself down onto the pillows Alex had placed beneath her and took a deep breath. The feeling of vulnerability when Alex's strong hands moved her legs apart caused her breath to hitch. Alex's hands gently caressed her sides, his fingertips lightly brushing along the sides of her breasts with each stroke; the rhythm was almost hypnotizing. Soon he had moved in close enough, the head of his cock was brushing against her pussy lips, and she knew her arousal was obvious since she was soaking wet.

"Well, it seems you are enjoying this new position, love. You're a natural submissive, you know. Your body knows what it wants. As you learn to embrace your submission, we'll be able to bring you to climaxes you'll think are going to shatter your soul. There will be a level of freedom in submission that will let you soar to the peaks of the highest mountains. By letting us lead you into ecstasy, you'll take us right along with you."

Running a finger along her slit to coat it with her juices, he used it to circle her puckered rosette, pressing just enough at its center to get her attention. At her quick intake of breath, he leaned over her.

"Someday soon—not tonight, you're not ready just yet, but soon—we'll fuck you here. You're going to love having us both inside you at the same time, baby."

"I–I don't know if I can do that. I'm afraid it's going to hurt too much. You are both so big, I don't think you'll fit."

"Oh, we'll make sure you're ready. It will hurt a bit the first couple of times, but I promise you, that edge of pain will make the pleasure so much greater. Now relax and let me love you." With that, Alex lined his cock up with her soft entrance and began his slow slide into her. She was relieved when he muttered about her feeling like heaven. "I knew you'd be tight, but I wasn't prepared for this feeling of absolute perfection. I'm going to remember this moment for the rest of my life."

KAT WAS TRYING to hold still, she really wanted to, but, oh God, the feel of Alex sliding his cock into her from this different angle was beyond description. She could already feel her pussy fluttering, she needed him to move, right now! When she tried to push back against him, his hands gripped her hips, stilling her.

"Oh no, love, hold still. I'm not going to be rushed. I've waited forever for this moment, and I'm going to savor it. Your pussy pulling me in, I don't even know words to describe how incredible that feels. You're wet and hot, your sheath is squeezing my cock so tight, the pleasure/pain is mind-numbing. At this moment, the only thing I can think about is this. I want you to let go of all thoughts and just feel."

Feeling every ridge and vein of Alex's cock was sending tiny sparks of awareness coursing through her entire body, and Kat was lost in a bliss she hadn't even known existed. She had no idea she could feel so possessed by a man when he wasn't even face-to-face with her. She'd been able to see Zach's expression while he'd loved her, but with Alex, it was all about losing herself in the timbre of his voice and the depths of his passion. He slowly began to move in and out in long, slow strokes; it was a tortuous ride to paradise. Each time she felt herself nearing the edge, he'd shift ever so slightly, and she'd start the slow climb again until every bit of her consciousness was centered on the mind-numbing pleasure he was bringing to her. Then without warning, he leaned over her and spoke directly in to her ear.

"Come for me, Katarina."

Her world was instantly awash in brilliant colors, and she felt as if she'd free fallen over the edge into oblivion. She felt him still and heard him shout her name before he pulled her close, clutching her to his chest in a grip so tight, she wasn't even sure she'd be able to draw in a breath. She let her eyes slide closed; she couldn't ever remember feeling this complete or this exhausted.

ENTERING KATARINA HAD been unlike anything he'd ever experienced. It felt like coming home, but at the same time, the adrenaline rush had been completely intoxicating. More than once, he'd simply held still and absorbed her warmth and the pleasure of being inside her. Alex and Zach had waited so long for this moment, and right now, he had no idea how he'd ever been so stupid to push her away. He couldn't fathom why he was being given a second chance, but in this moment, he only knew how eternally grateful he was.

Alex rolled to his side, taking Katarina with him after what had been the most powerful orgasm of his life. He'd known he wanted her, that his need to protect and keep her was stronger than anything he'd ever experienced, but this? This was something entirely foreign. This experience was life changing and he hadn't been prepared for it. Sure, his father had always told him the right woman would change his life between one heartbeat and the next, but he'd always thought that was poetic gibberish, not a factual description.

He held her close until he heard her breathing even out and knew she'd fallen asleep. Gently pulling from her body, he used the cloth Zach had given him to gently clean his seed from between her thighs and covered her with a soft blanket. Moving to the bathroom to clean himself up, he leaned against the counter, lost in thought when he heard Zach at the door.

"She's ours... we have to make sure she knows it, feels it to the bottom of her soul and that she believes she belongs here, with us, always." Zach's words echoed Alex's own thoughts as they often did.

"I agree. I don't even think there are words to describe the power she has over me. In some ways, it's almost frightening." Then with a small chuckle, he added, "I'm pretty sure this little bit of a sub is going to own us. Hell, she already holds our hearts in her hand."

Looking into his brother's eyes, Alex knew Zach felt exactly the same way. "We have to make sure she's safe, eliminate the threat against her before we can fully pursue the life we want to build. Alex turned to Zach, adding, "And we need to deal with our sister dearest. I can't tell you how frustrated I am with Jenna. I understand her need to honor Katarina's request for confidentiality, but Jenna knew what efforts we'd gone to in order to find Katarina. What on earth was she thinking, keeping this from us for so long?"

"I don't know, but I agree, we have to deal with her.

Honestly, I'm half tempted to let Colt handle it, he'd have more options. Hell, our only recourse is lecturing her, and God knows, she's immune to that." Smiling at the thought, he said, "When is she supposed to arrive? I was hoping she'd wait until after the beach party because I know it's going to be a battle to keep her out of it. And she wasn't always the best influence on Katarina."

"I agree, but I think she is scheduled to be here late tomorrow night, so we'll need to pull security from the party to keep an eye on the two of them. Keeping them away from the party is going to be difficult. Telling our little sister she can't do something has always been like waving a red flag in front of a bull." Stepping back into the bedroom, they both watched Kat sleeping peacefully for a few moments before switching off the lights and closing the door quietly as they left her room.

Chapter 11

JENNA WAS GLAD to be home even though the house she'd grown up in looked very little like it had when she was a kid. The mountains and forests were the same, and it was comforting to be surrounded by nature again. Living in the city was beginning to wear very thin. The ever-present noise and foul-smelling air were exhausting, and realizing nobody knew or cared anything about you was depressing. Jenna was drained and had been running on fumes far too long.

In the beginning, traveling had been one of the greatest things about her job; now, it just seemed like she was wasting her life away in airports, hotels, and rental cars. She was spending so much of her time *waiting*, she didn't have any left over to actually *live*. And she was worried about Kat. Her friend's last e-mail had been very odd and cryptic like she really hadn't been herself. When Jenna had asked about how her prick boyfriend was treating her, she hadn't gotten her usual graphic description of his latest 'the whole world revolves around me' antics. Instead, Kat's answer had been so completely out of character, Jenna had actually wondered if it had been written by someone else. And now all her calls to Kat's phone were going straight to voice mail; and Katarina was always diligent about keeping her phone near her.

Two days ago, when she'd called Alex to confirm her travel arrangements, she'd told him she was thinking about stopping in Las Vegas to check on a friend. His response had surprised her; he'd been adamant she return straight to ShadowDance. He hadn't seemed to care her unnamed friend might be in trouble. Hell, Mr. Up in Everybody's Business hadn't even asked who she'd be visiting, and that was also extremely unusual.

Having two older brothers would probably be a pain in the ass no matter what, but when those brothers were twins *and* ex-Special Forces—like anyone was ever really ex once they'd been a member of 'The Teams'—it was an exponential problem. Alex and Zach were also both Dominants which gave them the erroneous idea they were in charge of her. Lord, save her from her loving siblings. Not only did the two of them always believe they knew what was best for her—how she should dress and who she should associate with—now, they had a whole security team to enlist in their efforts to micromanage her life.

As she pulled up to the front of the house, the hair stood up on the back of her neck, and she briefly considered turning her car around and heading back to the airport. She'd always had great instincts when it came to trouble with the 'Dynamic Duo' as she'd often referred to her brothers, and for some reason, right now her internal alarm was pinging off the chart.

Sighing, she decided to put everything out of her mind for now. She'd try to contact Kat again tomorrow, but right now, she was just going to enjoy a little peace and quiet and let her brothers pamper her. Heck, that's what big brothers were supposed to do, right? Jenna got out of her car and headed up the wide stone steps, but knew the minute she saw both Alex and Zach standing with their arms crossed over their chests, scowling at her with what she'd always called their 'death glares,' she knew all was not well in Wonderland.

Jenna stopped a few steps below them and adopted a similar stance. "Well, I'm sure glad to see you both. Oh, yeah, welcome home, Jenna, we're just thrilled to see you, too. Thanks, big brothers mine, I'm overjoyed to be here!" She thought she might have seen just a twitch on Zach's lip, but Alex's expression didn't change. Looking past them, she saw Colt Matthews leaning in a deceptively casual pose against the railing surrounding the wraparound veranda. "Oh joy, joy, looks like the backup enforcer has come out to play as well." Jenna waited just a couple of seconds for a response and when they all continued to glare at her, she just skirted around them. "Well, I'm going to find Selita, I'm starving. Catch you all later."

"Jenna Beth. Office. Now." Alex's growl might frighten terrorists and all those international criminals they didn't think she knew they were still taking missions to track down, but not this little sister, nope, so not going to happen. She turned on him in a flash and stood with her toes up against his, shaking her finger up at him.

"Don't you try to intimidate me, Alexander Lamont. I'm not one of your little soldier boys or one of your Club flunkies or a sub you can just order around. You want to speak with me, you ask me like the gentleman Mama raised you to be. I don't take orders from you. Remember that, big brother." Turning to Zach, she added, "That goes for you, too." Then shifting her glare to Colt, she tacked on, "And it goes double for you, Colt Matthews. This is not going to end well, let me tell you. I've been traveling for the better part of the past twenty-four hours. I'm worried sick about a friend, tired, grimy, hungry, and just plain bitchy. So, you might want to choose your battles carefully."

Boy, she was on a roll. She didn't often let loose on them because ordinarily, she found it easier to work around their silly mandates, but this needed to stop. She was tired of everybody telling her what to do. Cripes, mostly she was just tired.

Colt stepped forward and grasped her elbow, pulling her back until she was facing him. "Well, princess, let's take this discussion into the office; there is no reason to involve the entire staff." He began leading her down the hall.

Alex and Zach looked on, momentarily shocked Colt had finally taken a stance with Jenna and even more surprised she'd allowed it. Alex was sure Zach was thinking the same thing he was. Hell, this battle might actually be fun to watch because it would be a battle of wills of epic proportions. Oh, they were both still seven kinds of pissed off at her, and they were damned well going to make sure she knew it, but now it looked like they might finally have some real help handling Jenna, allowing them to get back to their first priority, protecting Katarina.

Jenna let Colt usher her into the office. He sat her next to him on the very edge of the sofa, her posture rigid, arms crossed in defiance while her brothers each stood leaning against the fireplace, watching. Their casual poses were betrayed by the set of their jaws and narrowed eyes.

"Okay, now tell me what the hell this is about, so I can get something to eat and crash." Jenna was just about to get up and leave when Colt put his hand on her knee and squeezed. His message was clear…*Don't you dare move*. Well, this was sure fun. *Welcome home, Me!*

Chapter 12

C OLT TURNED HIS full focus on Jenna and watched her eyes dilate as a nice rosy flush colored her cheeks. Well, well, it would seem the lady wasn't as immune to him as she wanted him to believe. Interesting. Alex and Zach had asked him to take the lead with Jenna because they didn't think they'd be able to do it without losing their tempers, and they were neither one willing to give her the paddling she so richly deserved. Colt went straight for her throat.

"When is the last time you had any communication with Katarina McKay?" Oh yes, the joy of a surprise attack; Jenna stiffened slightly, blinked her eyes, and glanced down for a split second, but it was enough, he had her. "Don't even think about lying to me, Jenna." Colt's voice was low and menacing, he wanted her to know he'd tolerate nothing less than the absolute truth.

WELL CRAP, CRAP, crap. This a disaster of epic proportions. Not only was she worried sick about Kat, but now she was painted into a corner she knew there was no way out of. *Damn!* There wasn't a chance in hell that question had come out of the blue. She knew these three well enough to know if they were asking, they likely already had the answer.

"Well, I haven't spoken to her recently, if that's what you are implying." She gave herself a mental high five, she was ridiculously proud of that answer. It was the truth… of course, it was dependent upon how one chose to define 'recently' but still. She wasn't typically this good at semantics games when she was tired, so this was definitely a win. Fatigue also tended to have a very adverse effect on her tolerance for bullshit, so she was going to enjoy even the smallest victory right now.

As if he'd read her thoughts, Colt said, "Define *recently*."

Geez, what was he, some kind of flippin' mind reader? Christ, that kind of answer had always been golden with her parents. Of course, her mom and dad had always thought their youngest was the golden child which played heavily in her favor. Her brothers were tougher sells by far, and Colt looked positively pissed.

Sighing, Jenna played with a string on her short skirt, rolling it back and forth between her brightly polished nails. They knew she was stalling, and she knew they knew, but it didn't matter. They'd blindsided her, and she was sure that had been their plan. If she could only find out how much they knew, maybe she could walk away relatively unscathed.

"Why?" she asked, deciding to hedge. "Has something happened I should know about?" Alex took a step toward her, but Colt held up his hand to stop him. "Okay, okay, geez, talk about your anal control freaks. I've been talking to Kat for a while now." *Best not to give away the bank just yet.* "We've been e-mailing and Skyping, why?"

"You were aware your brothers had launched a full-out search after Katarina left Climax seven years ago, were you not?" At Kat's nod, he continued, "And you were aware they continued to search for her, putting out feelers as recently as last fall, were you not?"

Oh damn, this was not going well at all, she simply nodded her head again. Seriously, the man had obviously been watching too many old Perry Mason re-runs.

"And you were aware Katarina had recently become involved with someone who had threatened her safety on several occasions, and that he'd physically harmed her at least once that you'd gotten her to admit to, correct?"

Oh shit, to use one of her brothers' favorite expressions, she was officially up to her ass in alligators.

"Would you like to explain how you rationalized not relaying any of this information to your brothers? How could you have so little regard for your best friend's safety, you didn't bother to notify the two men you knew had been looking for her since the day she'd left ShadowDance Mountain? Why wouldn't you confide in the men you know would stop at nothing to protect her?"

Man, when he said it like that, keeping Kat's secret seemed like a pretty dumb idea. God, she had already been close to panic worrying about Kat, and now Colt had managed to toss her in to a pit of guilt that would surely make Sister Mary Margaret proud. Feeling her eyes fill with tears, Jenna looked up, and just as she opened her mouth to speak, she was cut short.

"That's quite enough, gentlemen. You have no right to make Jenna feel guilty for honoring a confidence I begged her to keep. She tried to get me to seek her family's help, but I was convinced I could handle it on my own. I've been taking care of myself for a very long time. Don't you dare blame her for the mess I've gotten myself into. If my being here is going to cause trouble in this family, I'll leave tonight." Kat stood in the doorway with her hands on her hips, glaring at all three men.

"Kitten, this doesn't involve you." Zach moved toward Kat. "Please, let me take you back upstairs. You need your rest."

Kat held her ground, shaking her head. Men just never ceased to amaze her. When they used sweet words and a gentle tone, they expected you to just blindly go along with whatever horse hockey they threw in your direction. *I don't think so, hot shot. I've learned a few things during the past seven years.*

"Zach, you know perfectly well that's bullshit. You and Alex are angry at Jenna because she knew where I was and didn't rat me out." Holding up her hand when they started to speak, she said, "No, that's the bottom line. Jenna didn't know I'd been injured in Vegas. We haven't spoken since before that happened. Leave her out of this. Please don't take away the one person who has always loved me and who always believed in me, even when those close to her didn't." Direct hit. She knew it was a low blow, but they had it coming, and she refused to feel guilty, well, not much anyway, at their tortured expressions.

Walking over to sit next to Jenna, Kat leaned forward and hugged her best friend. God, it felt good to have Jenna back close enough to touch. They had been as close as sisters for almost their entire lives, and if there was anything Kat needed now, it was the shoulder of a friend to lean on.

ALEX WATCHED KAT and Jenna leave the room talking animatedly about how they were going to sweet-talk their long-time cook and housekeeper, Selita, into making cookies at this late hour; all three men groaned. The woman the Lamont's all affectionately referred to as the Honduran Dynamo had lived in the United States since she'd been a young girl, but she had never fully mastered the language or the nuances of slang. Her version of a common saying was often as baffling as it was amusing. Since Selita lived inside the mansion, no one doubted the women would have no problem getting her to bake one of their favorite treats. It really was humbling to see how easily those two could manipulate everyone around them.

Jenna was the taller of the two, and she couldn't be much over five foot two. Both women were too smart for their own good with minds always knee-deep in their next great scheme. Yes, Alex was quite sure life at Shadow-Dance had just gotten a whole lot more challenging.

Chapter 13

"WELL, YOU REALLY handled Jenna, didn't you?" Zach chuckled, knowing Colt would be pissed for being cheated out of spanking her. The sparks coming out of Colt's eyes confirmed it, and knowing his friend as well as he did, it was a safe bet he wasn't finished with her comeuppance, as he called it. In all the years they'd known Colt, Zach couldn't remember a time the other man had let a woman gain the upper hand, but Kat and Jenna had both set him back on his heels. Yes, indeed, *The Colt and Jenna Show* looked to be shaping up as a source of great entertainment.

Alex had started to pace, his agitation growing with each pass. "Just what makes Jenna think this is in any way acceptable behavior? Damnit, I tried to tell Mom and Dad all their coddling was going to lead to trouble. Fucking hell, she is going to be the death of me. I shudder to think about all the crazy notions she'll fill Katarina's head with. Geez, they were bad enough as kids. I swear Lucy and Ethel have nothing on those two. You just wait and see if I'm not right."

Zach was biting the inside of his mouth to keep from smiling. He knew neither Alex nor Colt would appreciate him not joining the lynching, but Zach had always lived by the notion you could catch more flies with honey than vinegar. Oh, he believed in discipline, and he was going to be happy to set Kat's happy little ass on fire when she disobeyed them, but he also knew you could lose a few battles and still win the war.

Zach was as frustrated with Jenna as Alex was, but he also wondered why she hadn't trusted them enough to tell them about Kat. He damned well planned to make sure his opinion was crystal clear to his beloved younger sister, but he also knew dragging them all through sewage tonight wasn't going to solve anything. There was a large part of him that was just grateful they had been communicating, or it was likely Kat would have never returned to ShadowDance when she'd been hurt and was obviously still in danger.

"Let's head to the kitchen and make sure they understand a few things before we call it a night. I'm sure they're going to be up late catching up, and I don't want to wait around until the crack of noon when they roll out of bed tomorrow to have this conversation." Alex was already stomping down the hall with Colt hot on his heels.

Zach sighed, knowing that the honey method wasn't going to be happening anytime soon, and he was fairly certain Alex's approach was going to keep them both out of Kat's bed for the foreseeable future. *Fuck*. His only consolation was it looked like Colt would be going down on the same ship. Smiling to himself, he decided to make the best of the situation and enjoy the fireworks he was sure were coming.

Chapter 14

KAT AND JENNA had their heads poked so far inside the refrigerator, Alex was half afraid they were trying to crawl inside. God, they were giggling like the teens he remembered so well. How many nights had he lain awake in some godforsaken hellhole, thinking about Katarina in her next-to-nothing pajamas, prancing around this very same kitchen late at night, doing exactly this same thing? Jesus, talk about a déjà vu moment.

Alex knew he'd fallen for Katarina years ago, and even though he hadn't made love to her until today, no woman had ever captured his interest the way she did. There was a sparkle that always seemed to shine from inside her. He'd never met anyone who'd been immune to her charm. How she'd managed to hook up with an evil bastard like Calvin Robertson was a mystery he'd probably never understand. Christ, the man was a first-class ass and was being watched by a number of Uncle Sam's alphabet agencies for a wide variety of suspected criminal associations and activities.

After Cal Robertson's father retired, the organizations he headed had suddenly become much more profitable, and no one believed it was due to Cal's astute business decisions. The worst part was that Robertson didn't seem to hesitate to pull out all the stops when he thought it even appeared as if he'd been disrespected. No one on their team doubted Cal Robertson would view Katarina's escape as a betrayal of the first order.

They'd already asked Colt to send a man to Las Vegas to try to find Mia, the woman who had helped Katarina escape. If she hadn't already faced Robertson's wrath, it was sure to come. Hopefully, they'd get to her before Robertson's men did.

The kitchen in their home was huge, but it was also Selita's domain, and she made certain everybody respected what she considered hers. Selita had been with their family for so long Alex didn't even remember a time when she hadn't run their household with a command that would do a four-star general proud. No one crossed her more than once. The elderly woman was almost as wide as she was tall, which wasn't saying much since he was pretty sure she couldn't meet the height requirement for most of the rides at an amusement park. When his parents had hired her, they'd built her a beautiful suite of rooms near the kitchen, and she'd lived with them ever since.

His father had always been evasive about how she'd come to them; all Alex had ever been able to learn was that she'd had an abusive husband who had almost killed her. Their parents had come across her lying in the street and stepped in to help. They'd offered her a job after she'd gotten out of the hospital, and she'd quickly become a member of their family. Selita eventually won over everyone she met—she might run over you first, but sooner or later you'd end up being her friend.

She kept the house in pristine condition, cooked mountains of food daily, and was always willing to lend an ear when someone needed a shoulder to lean on or just wanted to vent their frustrations about their rotten day. Selita had been a surrogate mother to not only him and his siblings, but to each of their employees as well. And now? Well, now she was scurrying around making sandwiches and snacks for 'her girls' like he'd seen her do so many times before.

At Katarina's mention of needing to go clothes shopping, he was brought back to the present. "You'll both remain here, meaning you will not even leave the house without having one of us or a member of the security team with you. You can order anything you need, and have it delivered." Kat and Jenna both turned to glare at him before he continued, "We haven't been able to locate Calvin Robertson yet, so Katarina still isn't safe. Jenna, your association with Katarina was being monitored by Robertson's techies, so he's likely to make an appearance here as soon as he realizes you've returned home."

"Oh my God, look what I've done! I've brought so much trouble to you all. It was selfish of me to even think of coming here." Alex looked up at his brother and could see Kat's look of defeat nearly undid him as well.

"No, Katarina, the only mistake you made was not contacting us sooner—well, that and going to the blasted lake instead of coming to the house. We'll be discussing that in the future, as well. Don't think we've forgotten about that, kitten." Zach had been leaning against the door, watching, so quiet Kat had almost forgotten he was there. Colt was also standing back; he seemed content to let Alex take the lead, but his body language fairly shouted that he was not going to bend on this at all.

Taking a deep breath to try to help bite back her immediate response, Kat said, "Well, that's all well and good, but there are things I need right away, things that I'd rather choose personally. If I order from any of the local stores, you know they'll have someone go pick things off the shelf, and do you really want some high school boy picking out my panties?" When she heard Zach groan and Alex growl, she knew her comments had hit their mark.

"Make a list of what you need, Zach or I will personally pick up everything. There will not be anyone else making undergarment selections for you, is that clear? You'll need a variety of clothing as well. Who purchased the clothing that was in your car?" Alex was fairly certain he knew the answer to that question since most of the items had tracking devices imbedded in the seams, but he needed to be sure.

"I didn't have a chance to pick up much from my apartment, and what I brought was all I could find quickly. That's odd, too, now that I think about it, all the things I could find were items Cal had bought for me." Kat seemed to think about that for a second before continuing. "Wait. Why? What's wrong with the clothes I brought?"

Colt stood up and moved forward saying, "Everything you brought with you had tracking chips, so no matter where you were, Robertson's security office in Los Angeles was able to track you to within a few feet via satellite. From what we've been able to find out so far, he's been doing this for some time, at least a few weeks. It's a miracle you made it here before they caught up with you. And you can be sure they are close now. They've already made attempts to bypass the electronic monitoring on the property's perimeter, unsuccessfully I might add. But don't think they've given up. And when not if they come calling, we'll be ready." *

Chapter 15

ALEX TOOK SEVERAL quick steps forward, stepping in front of Katarina just as her knees buckled. He'd seen her start to shake when Colt had laid out the danger she was facing and watched the blood draining from her face quickly as fear steamrolled her. Carrying her to the nearest chair, he sat down and settled her on lap.

"Katarina, look at me." When she finally looked up, Alex smoothed the blonde strands of her hair away from her face. "You are safer here than any place else you could possibly be. Everything you brought with you has either had the chips removed or has been destroyed. We'll return your computer to you just as soon as we can, but right now we're using it as a backdoor into their system. Remember, love, this is what we do. Please don't worry—that's our job. You need to recover, and we'd like you and Jenna to stay together during the day as much as possible, it will help us protect you both."

Kat started to calm; Alex's voice always had the ability to soothe her, its deep timbre and measured cadence was a balm to her soul. He was rubbing his hand in small circles ever so lightly on her lower back, and she felt the tension draining from her taut muscles. She knew Cal was more than she could fight alone. She'd never been able to understand his obsession with her. He could have his pick of women why did he want her? She finally laid her head against Alex's shoulder and let him wrap his arms around her. She hadn't realized how much she needed just to be held; the comfort of his embrace was all she could think about at this moment, everything else was just too much.

Colt turned his attention to Jenna. "You will need to stay inside at all times unless you have a security escort. This is nonnegotiable, Jenna, so don't even try any of your shenanigans. Don't give me that wide-eyed, innocent look, it won't work. I know you too well, princess. And don't think we won't know, we will, and there will be consequences for noncompliance."

Zach stepped forward then, and said, "We have a special event for The Club this weekend. There will be a lot of guests coming and going. We have stepped up the security protocols, but there is always the chance Robertson can get to someone who has already been cleared to attend. You both need to remain inside the house and away from the windows at all times. We don't want any of the guests knowing either one of you are here."

What he didn't say was that none of them wanted either Kat or Jenna to see any of the activities either. Not that they didn't both know what kinds of things happened at The Club, but they certainly weren't seeing anything without their men being with them. And even though Jenna and Colt might not have accepted it, it was clear to everyone around them, she belonged to him.

JENNA WAS PISSED, well and truly off-the-chart angry. "Consequences for noncompliance?" What the hell? Who did Colt think he was talking to, one of his underlings? Damn, even Zach had just waved a red flag at her, and he was usually the reasonable one of this group of Neanderthals. Zach had just made spying on their big weekend *event* her number one priority, the big idiot. *They must be planning one hell of a party if they don't want either us to see what was going on.*

Giving them her sweetest smile, she demurred. "Okay, we'll do whatever we need to so we're safe. We don't want to make it any more difficult for your security staff than it needs to be that's for sure." *Right, we don't want you to think you need to assign extra bozos to babysit us. Hopefully, you'll think we're being cooperative and won't send your best guys, and we'll be able to work around them.*

NOT ONE SINGLE person in the room believed Jenna's little performance, Oscar-worthy as it was. Christ, the woman would test the patience of a saint. Colt leaned forward, letting her think she'd pulled one over on them, because he was certain it would work in their best interest.

"Thanks, we appreciate your cooperation. We'll be assigning staff to the house, but it will be a relief to know we don't have to worry about you trying to work against us." *Touché, sweetheart, two can play your game.* Colt watched as Alex slid an arm beneath Katarina's knees and picked her up as he stood.

"Jenna, you go ahead and get something to eat, then Colt will bring you up to Katarina's suite if you want to say good night to her before going to your room. I think she's done for the evening. Zach and I are going to take her upstairs and make sure she gets into bed. She needs to rest, she is still recovering both physically and emotionally. I don't want her overdoing it, her health and safety are our priority." Before Jenna or Kat could voice any protest, he turned and strode from the room. Zach followed them the through the living room and up the curving staircase.

KAT'S SUITE WAS really a moderately sized apartment; including a sitting room, a small kitchenette, an enormous bathroom, along with a huge bedroom featuring a bed specifically designed to be comfortable for two very large men and Kat. The suite took up the entire end of the second floor of the mansion wing and featured an outdoor deck, complete with a hot tub, outdoor bar, and fireplace. The deck wrapped around two sides, offering a panoramic view of the mountains that remained snowcapped year-round.

The view of the surrounding forests looked like something from a travel brochure, and they knew Kat had noticed the deck offered great views of the newly renovated gardens, allowing her a chance to enjoy the view of the landscaping and beauty of The Club's newest feature without her being privy to all the activities occurring there. It wasn't that they wouldn't be having their own fun with her in the gardens, but confidentiality was one of their Club's hallmarks, and who knew what a visitor might be able to see from the deck someday. Alex and Zach had both shuddered at the thought of any breach of security. Alex had helped the architect who was a Club member, so the suite was as safe as they'd been able to make it.

When they'd decided to build a BDSM club, they'd looked at several local sites before deciding that adding it as a second wing to the existing mansion gave them some unique advantages. The second wing provided an enclosure, a protected area they had been able to turn in to a garden paradise. It butted up against the forest on two sides, which provided shelter from Mother Nature as well as a beautiful backdrop to the gardens. The pools and streams were heated by naturally occurring hot springs in the area, and the constantly circulating water kept the temperature in the gardens at a tolerable level, even in the most extreme Colorado winter weather, and during the summer, it felt almost tropical.

The road leading up to ShadowDance was the only access for regular vehicles and they had improved on the security measures their father had implemented years ago. Now, no one using that road was able to get within five miles of the front gates without everyone on the security team knowing they were approaching. Each member of the security team was assigned an electronic marker and carried a small, state-of-the-art handheld device which not only showed the location of everyone who was tagged, but also showed any hostiles. Anyone who wasn't supposed to be there was considered a hostile until proven otherwise. Hell, they'd known Jenna was on the road long before she'd called to say she was approaching the front gates.

BOTH ALEX AND Zach knew it was going to be difficult to convince Katarina and Jenna of the importance of them being completely compliant with the restrictions they were being forced to follow. Alex and Zach had learned at an early age about the importance of security from the Lamont patriarch, Daniel Lamont. Their father had always known his family was a security risk.

As a well-known, wealthy entrepreneur who seemed to have a Midas touch, their dad had heard too many horror stories from other men in his business and social circles about their wives and children being targeted because of their families' wealth. Their dad had taken what many had seen as extraordinary measures to ensure the safety of his own family. As a result, Alex and Zach had gotten a head start on their knowledge of surveillance technology, which had been very useful when they'd earned places in the Special Forces teams.

Their parents now lived in a beautiful condo in Denver when they weren't traveling the world, but they both still made themselves available any time any of their children needed help. All three of the Lamont children felt like their parents had more than earned this time, and none of them liked to impose if it wasn't absolutely necessary.

Alex couldn't help but smile when he thought about how his father worshipped their beautiful mother. Catherine Lamont was a gorgeous former model with a keen mind for business. Her intelligence always seemed to surprise people because more often than not, they underestimated the beautiful blonde. It was a mistake they usually regretted quickly, and she always managed to use their lapses to her advantage.

Catherine Lamont had been a huge factor in her husband's success, but more importantly, she'd always openly returned her husband's devotion. She had never felt stifled by his efforts to shield her, even when she'd been criticized both personally and professionally for not setting a good example as an *independent woman*. Their parents' obvious love and respect for each other had set a high standard by which Alex, Zach, and Jenna would always measure their own relationships.

When Alex had spoken to his father earlier today, he'd been thrilled his sons were finally going after the woman everyone had always known was perfect for them. His sage advice was demonstrating love in a thousand small ways always outweighed garish displays. Alex had vowed to himself yet again that he'd spend his life making sure Katarina was showered with the kind of love and attention he'd watched his father bestow on his mother. It would always be his duty and privilege to make sure she was always safe and felt confident and secure enough to explore every facet of her sexuality. *Yes indeed, from the looks of things, the next sixty or seventy years might not always be smooth sailing, but they are never going to be dull.*

Chapter 16

K AT SAT ON the floor of the sitting room in her suite, watching the fire in the stone fireplace flicker while she sipped one of the mega-margaritas she and Jenna had made. She was lost in thought as they considered how they were going to escape the prison they'd been locked in. Hell, the Feds' most secure facilities didn't have much on the lockdown Alex and Zach, along with Warden Colt as Jenna had nicknamed him, had imposed on them.

In the back of her mind, Kat knew the margaritas were probably a bad idea, but at this moment, she was so frustrated, she just couldn't seem to make herself care. Jenna had always had a much higher alcohol tolerance than she did, and Jenna's tolerance was lame compared to most people.

The two of them had gotten in quite a lot of trouble over the years, and the worst of those incidents always seemed to occur after consuming various umbrella-decorated, fruity concoctions that seemed to sneak up and bite you in the ass when you least expected it. Damn, this had to be the best margarita she'd ever had, but somehow her glass always seemed to be empty... odd that.

"I don't know, we maybe should take it easy with these," Jenna said, holding up her now-empty glass. "But then again... well, shit, would you look at that, mine's empty, too. No worries, we made plenty. Here, I have the pitcher right here, give me your glass." Filling both of their glasses with the showmanship of a world-class bartender, Jenna giggled, "Wow, did you see that? Damn, I'm good, you should be congratulating me for only spilling a little on the carpet. Shit, I'll have to remember to clean that up before Alex sees it. He's so anal about that stuff.

"So, whadda ya think our odds of breakin' outta this joint is, I mean are?" Jenna didn't pause long enough for Katarina to answer. "Frack, maybe I'd better watch my margarita intake a little closer, that didn't really sound like me. And did somebody just tilt the room to the right?"

"Blast if I know, did you see they have two yoyos out on the deck and outside the door? And who knows how many others are hiding in the house. Damn and double damn. Ya know, I wasn't all that keen on spying on their damned party until they banned us. Just who do they thing, I mean think, they are tellin' us whad, oops, what we can and can't do, anyhow?" The indignation she'd intended seemed to be negated by the giggle she'd let bubble to the surface. Oh well, Jenna would know Kat had meant to sound righteous—damn, that was funny… *righteous*… what a funny word. She fell in to a fit of giggles that soon had Jenna giggling, too. It took them several minutes to get themselves back under control.

"We need to work on our 'scape plan, we can do this… probably. We're smart women, those Barney wannabes got nuttin' on us! Hell, I'll bet Alex plus two didn't even give 'em any bullets. Hell, Zach used to be the sweet one, and now he's acting just like Alex, that really sucks, I tell ya'. And that Colt is a whole new level of grim. He doesn't like me, you know? Have you ever actually seen him smile? Maybe it's some sort of genetic defect. He might be bigger than me, but I'm mouthy and fast, and that's almost as good as all that fancy-assed training he's had, right?" Kat's words were followed by another chorus of giggles before they finally seem to recover a bit.

"Yeah, sister, we can outsmart 'em... don't ya think? I mean really, just because they fought against terrorists, doesn't mean they're smarter than us!" Somewhere in the very back of Jenna's mind, she knew they were so busted, but it just didn't seem as important as it had an hour ago.

LISTENING TO THE woman discuss their plans to spy on The Club's Beach Party, the guys in the security monitoring command center, known as the Crow's Nest, were having a great time eavesdropping and watching as the women hatched a plan that would have been doomed to go down in flames even without their alcohol-fogged thinking. There were always at least two people working the bank of monitors in the Crow's Nest and usually, three during events. The Club's security center was Mitch Grayson's domain, he was considered the lead for most events, and this evening was no different. He'd been calling Alex, Zach, and Colt with regular updates, well, when he could do so without letting his amusement at the women's antics be heard in his voice.

Grayson had been instructed to place monitoring equipment in the sitting room for this evening; it seemed Alex and Zach knew their sister and Ms. McKay very well, indeed. They'd said they were sure the two wildcats, as they'd referred to them, would not be easily contained. And as entertaining as this had been, their increasing inebriation was starting to cause some concern. It was probably getting close to time to call in the cavalry.

ORDINARILY, THE SUITE only had perimeter-monitoring devices out of respect for her privacy, but Kat knew full well Alex and Zach would have stepped that up for tonight. The Lamont brothers were worried about the two of them getting out of their gilded cage, but she knew they were even more worried about who might get in. On any other day, that might have been valuable information, but right now, Kat was feeling like it just didn't really matter all that much that there might be 'bad guys' out there. Why were there bad guys after her? Damned if she could remember, she'd probably just dreamed that part.

Looking over at her best friend, Kat noticed the room seemed to move way too fast when she turned her head too quickly. *What was that about anyway? I can fix that, I'll just move really, really slow.*

"Ya know, I'll bet we could go down to the big kitchen and get some munchies, they'd let us do that, dontcha think? And that would get us closer to the gardens. And those are closer to The Club. Damn and double damn, but I want to see what Pervs-R-Us has going on out there, too. Those guys on the deck are blockin' our view."

KAT AND JENNA got to their feet and each had to grab onto the mantle to keep from toppling into the fire. Mitch

Grayson sighed and hit the button on the console that would connect him to the three men he'd been reporting to throughout the evening. Yep, definitely time to bring in reinforcements.

Chapter 17

HITTING THE BUTTON on the side of his headset, Colt simply said, "Talk to me." He'd been standing right next to Alex and Zach and seen their com-units blink at the same time his activated and knew full well the only person who would be interrupting all three of them was Mitch Grayson.

"Boss, they're on the move, well, sort of…"

"What the fuck do you mean by *sort of?*" Colt barked in to his unit.

"Well, they're pretty toasted, and when they got up off the floor, they both had trouble maintaining position, sir." Mitch found himself reacting predictably to Colt's tone, which always put the entire security team right back into their military mind-set. Their communication became much more formal and cryptic as a result. Alex and Zach had commented they had both noticed the same response in themselves, and all three assumed as long as they were still *freelancing* for Uncle Sam, the habit wasn't likely to fade anytime soon.

"Well, fuck!" they all three responded at the same time, bringing a smile to Mitch's face he was grateful they couldn't see. "We'll be right up. Make sure they don't leave the suite." Colt disconnected before Mitch could respond. Studying the video feed, Mitch watched as the three men turned as one and headed to Katarina's suite. He could see they were bracing themselves for the confrontation they had to know was coming. They'd made it just a few steps when they heard a rifle shot and the shattering of glass, followed by a heart-stopping scream.

"HOLY SHIT, WHAT was that?" Jenna turned when she heard shattering glass and stumbled to regain her footing just in time to watch Kat's eyes go wide as she sank to the floor. Jenna watched in horror as blood spread across Kat's chest. She heard a scream and realized it came from her. Kat was sprawled on the floor, her eyelids slowly drifting closed.

Jenna finally got her feet to cooperate and moved to Kat's side. She crouched low, covering Kat's body with her own just as the door to the suite crashed open and men dressed in black came in from the hall as well as through the now-shattered glass doors leading to the deck. She batted away hands that tried to move her out of the way, but soon felt strong arms wrap around her waist from behind and lift her away from Kat's side.

"No, she needs me. Put me down, you oaf! Somebody, call my brothers! Oh my God, Kat! Don't you dare die on me! I just got you back... don't you dare leave me again!" Jenna was nearing total meltdown when she was turned and came face-to-face with the grim expression of Colt Matthews.

"Goddamn it, Jenna, settle down. Stopping fighting me and stay back so we can help her. Stay put, we need to secure the area and get to Katarina. Let us work, please!" None of Colt's words had any impact, but his heartfelt *please* stunned her into silence.

Okay, things were even worse than she thought if he actually said please. Jenna stayed in the chair where Colt had set her. If she really wanted to help her friend, she needed to stay out of way and let the professionals do everything they could to save her. Even though she still felt a bit foggy, she was a whole lot more sober now than she'd been five minutes ago. Holding herself perfectly still, she started praying to a God she hadn't talked to in way too long. She made all the usual promises, including vows to try to follow instructions given by the security team... well, at least until after Kat was safe.

THE LEFT SIDE of Kat's chest and her shoulder felt like it was on fire. Damn, something must have bitten her. *Fuck a duck, I hate it when shit bites me. And what is all that noise?* Geez, if she could just get her eyes open, she could figure out what the hell was going on. Where had all these people come from? Even though she couldn't see them, she could hear them. And were those sirens she was hearing? This had to be the weirdest dream she'd ever had, and she'd had some doozies. Swearing she'd never drink Jenna's margaritas again if she got out of this crazy dream, Kat felt Alex and Zach touch her and knew it was okay to just let herself slide back into the sweet oblivion of sleep. They'd take care of it, whatever it was... Yeah, she'd just take a little nap, and it would all be gone soon.

"SHIT, SHE'S LOSING a lot of blood! Where the fuck are those paramedics with that equipment?" Zach had been their team's medic, so he'd grabbed his med-kit as he'd sprinted past his room, but it didn't have everything he needed. Christ, he knew it was a through-and-through injury, and based on the entrance and exit wounds, he was fairly certain it hadn't done any major damage, but they wouldn't know for sure without getting her to a hospital quickly. He couldn't ever remember being this scared.

There just wasn't that much he could do besides keeping pressure packs on Kat's chest and back until he had more to work with. Jesus Christ, someone had shot her! If she'd been steady on her feet, he had no doubt the bastard's shot would have gone straight through her heart. They'd have lost her before she ever hit the floor. Even though the alcohol had likely saved her by making her unsteady, it was also making her bleed a lot more than she would have any other time. "Those paramedics need to get up here, right fucking now!"

ALEX WAS SHOUTING orders to their security team, getting them headed up the mountain to see if the shooter had left anything behind; he was certain the bastard was long gone by now. Thank God Kat and Jenna had been sitting on the floor. If they'd been on the sofa, the guy would have had a clear shot much earlier. The way it was, he'd had to take a shot when Katarina got to her feet, and the fact that she'd faltered had been her saving grace.

He'd been more than a little annoyed all evening as the reports of their increasing intoxication made their way to the three of them, but he sure wasn't going to be complaining about it now. He could see Zach working to stop the bleeding and had seen the signal his brother had flashed earlier, letting him know the injury wasn't life threatening, but she was still losing a lot of blood.

When Colt announced the paramedics were making their way up the front staircase, he'd immediately started clearing a path for them. Colt had gotten Jenna out of the way, and she was sitting like a statue; they'd need to assess her for shock right away as well. To use one of their team's favorite expressions, this had gone completely FUBAR—fucked up beyond all recognition—in a heartbeat. Jesus, they'd sworn they'd protect her, they'd promised her she'd be safe if she just stayed in her suite. The only thing keeping him from feeling like a total failure was his determination to make the son of a bitch responsible pay and pay in a big way. Calvin Robertson had just signed his own death warrant as far as Alex was concerned—a sentiment he was quite sure his brother would second.

Chapter 18

T HE CLIMAX HOSPITAL might be small, but it was as technologically advanced and well-equipped as most big city trauma centers thanks to the generous donations of the Lamont family. Those donations had been made to help the entire community, but Alex had never dreamed how grateful he and Zach would be for their parents' generosity.

Doc Woods met them in the ER. The man might be old, but he'd seen it all. He had Kat poked, prodded, scanned, and stitched up in no time. She'd been moved into a private room and was sleeping peacefully, despite all the activity around her, no doubt compliments of the powerful pain meds Doc had given her.

Nurse Ratchet as the men had nicknamed her, had eventually threatened to throw them all out if they didn't move their "loud-mouth selves" to the waiting room. Wicked woman was really starting to piss Alex off, and the worst part was she didn't seem to be intimidated by him at all. *What the fuck?* He must be seriously losing his touch, first Jenna and now this nurse. Finally, Dylan Marshall, the local sheriff, interceded and led her off down the hall.

Dylan was currently charming her with that bogus Texas good ole boy routine he'd perfected when he'd done so much undercover work during his time with the DEA.

His name was an endless source of embarrassment for Dylan and had provided his friends with hours of teasing material when they'd been kids. Their teasing had reached a fever pitch when Dylan had decided to follow his dad into law enforcement. To this day, just the mention of the television show *Gunsmoke* wound him up like an eight-day clock.

After several years with the DEA, Dylan left the agency just as his dad decided he'd had enough and wouldn't be running for sheriff again. Technically, the investigation into the shooting would be under his jurisdiction, but Alex knew Dylan would be happy to work with them; they had resources his local budget wouldn't ever support, and they weren't limited by probable cause, warrants, etc. The thought they'd be able to pull together information which wasn't available through legitimate sources was the first thing in hours that had brought Alex anywhere near a smile.

ZACH STOOD BY Kat's bed, holding her small hand in his and thanked God, *again,* for another chance with her. She looked like a sleeping flower sprite, long blonde curls framing her sweet face on the pillow. She was still too pale, but with the transfusions and IVs, she was finally beginning to regain some color in her cheeks. She stirred, but settled again when he brushed the backs of his fingers down the side of her face; she responded to both him and Alex even in her sleep. He considered her unconscious response a sure sign she belonged to them; now, they just had to make sure she knew it on a conscious level as well.

Alex was haunted by their failure to protect her, but Zach wasn't going to waste even one moment of his time with her focusing on regret. His brother would come to the same conclusion, it would just take him a little time. Alex had always taken his role as the oldest—even though he was only two minutes older than Zach—way too seriously in Zach's opinion. Alex moved back inside Kat's room and handed a duffle to Zach.

"Here, go clean up and get changed, you don't want her to wake up and see you like that." Alex nodded to Zach's clothing which was covered in Katarina's blood. Zach passed her hand to him; it was a symbolic move and its significance wouldn't be lost on Alex. Taking the bag, Zach moved silently out of the room.

ALEX HAD JUST spoken with Doc Woods, ensuring Katarina's name would not appear in any hospital records. Even though her location had already been compromised, one of the things he knew was there was never any reason to hand your adversary information you didn't specifically want them to know. She'd told them Robertson had made it very clear that he felt she belonged to him. Knowing the man would rather see her dead than with someone else was almost more than Alex could comprehend.

"Katarina, love, you need to open those beautiful blue eyes. Doc Woods said you will be released into our care as soon as you wake up and he gets a last 'look-see' to quote the old fart." Alex was fond of the elderly doctor who'd been a fixture in Climax for as long as he could remember. Hell, he'd delivered most of the town's current residents.

Doc had always claimed they'd built the town around him, and Alex wasn't altogether sure that was an exaggeration.

Alex had assured Doc they'd be providing Katarina with round-the-clock medical care, and despite the fact she'd been shot while in their home, it would be much easier to secure her at ShadowDance than it would be in a public hospital.

"Katarina, you are racking up a lot of punishments, my beautiful sub, don't think we aren't keeping count. Now, I've given you an order, I expect you to follow without hesitation. Open your eyes for me, love."

Something in Alex's voice must have pulled her back up to the surface of consciousness. Her eyes fluttered open, and she blinked at the bright light above her bed. Alex quickly dimmed the light and smiled down at her. God, he was so relieved to have her awake. He'd lost ten years off his life when he'd heard that rifle shot. The few seconds it had taken them to sprint up to her suite had been the longest of his entire life.

If she thought they'd been overprotective before, she was about to find out just how restrictive they could be when it concerned her safety. "Welcome back, sweetheart. Glad to see you decided to rejoin us." Alex's voice nearly cracked with emotion, he was so incredibly overwhelmed by the way she was looking at him as if he had all the answers. God, he loved her so much.

Of all the things Alex had expected Katarina to say, her whispered "I'm so sorry" would never have even made the list.

"What?" Disbelief at what he'd heard had him asking, "Katarina, what on earth do you have to be sorry for? We're the ones who failed to protect you! Zach and I are the ones who should be begging your forgiveness. Oh, love, please don't cry. Tell me what you think you have done wrong." Alex was being completely undone by her tears, he couldn't imagine what she was thinking.

"I've brought you nothing but trouble. I really need to leave Climax before someone I care about is hurt because I was selfish enough to come here. Please, just let me go so you and your family are safe. I could never forgive myself if something happened to one of you because of me."

Alex could see she was fighting a losing battle to hold back her tears. He'd overheard her tell Jenna once how much she hated crying. Even as a teen, she'd understood the importance of maintaining control of her life.

"I don't know how I've managed to make so many bad decisions.? The only solution is to leave. I won't lie, it's going to break my heart into a million pieces, but if it will keep you safe, it will be worth it."

"Not happening, love. Now, let's see what we can do about getting you out of here." And with that, Alex turned and was out the door, cutting off any protests his beautiful Katarina might have voiced.

Chapter 19

K AT STOOD IN front of the glass doors leading to the gardens, hugging her arms around her. It was a gesture of comfort more than an indication of being cold, but Zach stepped up behind her, wrapping his arms around her.

"Cold, kitten?"

"No, just thinking."

"Talk to me, sweetheart, what's bothering you?" Zach had always been the more approachable of the two brothers, but Kat wasn't sure she could even explain how she was feeling.

"I guess I'm just suffering from cabin fever. I've been out of the hospital for a week, and I haven't even been allowed outside, much less off ShadowDance Mountain." Kat knew she was going to start jabbering again, but she just couldn't seem to stop it. "There hasn't been any indication I'm still in danger, and Jenna's gone back to work somewhere in bum-fuck Egypt, and you and Alex are busy all the time, and you won't let me go to The Club with you, and I'm bored out of my mind. You don't even want to sleep with me; it's the scars isn't it?" By the time she'd stopped for a breath, Kat was almost in tears. Emotionally, she was still reeling, but she didn't dare mention that or she'd never get to leave the house.

Sighing softly in resignation, she added, "Can I at least get my computer back? If I could work that would help. Besides, I need to put the finishing touches on a couple of projects for clients, so I can get paid. I need to get back to work, so I can find an apartment in town. I'll need money to start over. I'm sure my studio in Vegas has been picked clean by now. It wasn't exactly in the best neighborhood. The only reason I hadn't been robbed before was I worked from home and rarely left for more than an hour or two at a time. Anyway... I can't just stay here and live off you and Alex, I've intruded long enough. Do you suppose you could bring my car up front sometime today?"

Kat hadn't missed Zach's arms tightening around her as she spoke, and she knew neither he nor Alex was going to be happy with her decision to move out, but she really needed to get back to work, and if they weren't going to let her out of the house, she didn't think she'd be able to take being cooped up much longer.

Zach turned her around, so she was facing him, pushing a lock of hair behind her ear, and kissed her forehead.

"No, kitten, I'm afraid I can't do that. You're wrong if you think we don't want to sleep with you, nothing could be further from the truth. We knew you needed to rest and heal, and there was no way we could sleep with you and not spend the entire night inside you.

"As for the scars, you're going to be in a lot of trouble for thinking we're so shallow we'd see those rather than the beautiful woman you are. I'll be adding *that* to the rather long list of punishments you have coming, kitten.

"Let's see what we can do about getting you some fresh air, what do you say? Why don't you head upstairs and change clothes? Wear a sundress and nothing else. I'll pack us a picnic and we'll find a nice, secluded, sunny spot in the gardens." He waggled his eyebrows suggestively, and despite her best efforts, Kat giggled. Leave it to Zach to soften his refusal to bring her car up to the house with a promise of some quality time together. As Kat headed up the stairs, Zach speed dialed Alex. "Seems our woman is in need of some attention. Meet us at the waterfall in twenty."

KAT LOVED THE feel of the sunshine on her face; God, it felt good to be outside again. Walking hand in hand with Zach along the stone path that meandered through the gardens, she enjoyed seeing all the hidden elements of The Club's newest feature. She loved discovering all the little things tucked into small alcoves. There were a lot of benches in secluded spots, and she'd felt her cheeks flush when she noticed they all had rings imbedded in them, for restraints no doubt.

Smiling to herself, she thought about how it had felt the night Alex and Zach had restrained her. Rather than frightening her like it had with Cal, she'd found it thrilling with the Lamonts. She saw several things she wasn't familiar with, but decided it was probably wise to keep that information to herself for now. Kat had also noticed a lot of electronic monitoring and security equipment. The devices weren't always easy to spot, but it was obvious the safety of their members was a Club priority. She heard the sound of rushing water just before they rounded a corner, and Kat saw a stunning waterfall made of natural stone. Water rushed over the top before cascading into the pool below. It was truly breathtaking; she stood rooted in place staring in wonder, completely captivated.

"So, what do you think, kitten?" Zach had turned so he could see her reaction, and she didn't think he'd been disappointed because she was frozen in place by the beauty before her. Kat was sure her stunned look of awe told him how much she liked the gardens' centerpiece feature.

"The look on your face makes all the frustration we faced getting this one piece of the project completed worth it. The wonder in your eyes makes all the challenges pale in comparison. Come on, I want you to see the reflecting pool." He tugged on her hand until she followed him to the water's edge.

"I hope you still like to swim, the water is kept at the perfect temperature year-round, and I'm told the bubbles created by the waterfall add a little extra to the experience." His sexy grin told her he knew exactly what that 'little extra' was, too. "As soon as I get this blanket spread out, I want to check to see that you followed my directions. Since you mentioned going to The Club, I thought we spend this afternoon making sure you're ready for that experience."

As he spread out a blanket she hadn't even seen him pick up, he continued talking. "Because you are ours, there will be some members who will have particularly high expectations for you, so we want to make sure you are fully prepared. Remember, there are strict rules that need to be followed. We don't want you to be inadvertently put in a position where you could be punished by another Dom—we don't share well." Zach's smile might have looked easygoing, but the look of possession in his eyes told Kat he was quite serious. She tried to suppress the cold shiver of fear that ran up her spine at the thought of anyone but Alex or Zach touching or, God forbid, punishing her.

Chapter 20

K AT STOOD TO the side of the blanket, arms down to her sides while Zach walked around her slowly.

"You need to get used to being inspected, kitten. It will always be our right to view what is ours. This afternoon is going to be about making sure you fully understand what an evening at The Club might look like. Now, remove your dress, move your feet shoulder-width apart, and leave your hands at your sides."

Moving back several steps, Zach stood with his bulging arms crossed over his chest, feet apart, watching her intently. Kat looked so anxious, he had to resist the urge to smile. While he didn't want her to be afraid, a little apprehension would enhance her sensations and the experience in general. He'd noticed her looking around to be sure they were alone, and he was sure she'd noticed the cameras they used for surveillance.

Zach didn't intend to tell her he'd called the Crow's Nest before they'd left the house and had Grayson shut down this sector. She'd need to be as proud of her body as they were, she'd often be in various stages of undress while at The Club. He knew she was still very self-conscious of the lash marks on her back, many of them hadn't fully faded, and now she'd added the wounds from the rifle shot. Even though Doc Woods had done an amazing job of stitching her up, the scars on her chest and back were still red and angry looking against skin that reminded him of ivory satin. "Kitten, hesitating will get you punished. Remove the dress, *now*."

BOY OH BOY, *this is it.* Taking a deep breath, Kat slowly lifted the dress over her head and laid it aside. Spreading her legs apart as Zach had told her to, she took a deep breath and tried to pull herself back from the edge of panic.

"What were my instructions to you, kitten?" Zach asked, one eyebrow raised.

"Um, you said to wear a sundress. This is the only sundress I had, isn't it okay?" Kat was nervous because he didn't look happy, and she wasn't sure what she'd done wrong.

"Actually, my instruction was to wear a sundress and nothing else. I knew you left the house with your shoes on. Ordinarily, I'd have taken your shoes, and you'd have been punished before we left. Instructions are to be followed to the letter, kitten. Now, what else is wrong with this picture? Hmm?"

"I wasn't supposed to wear panties? Oh, my God, Zach, I can't run around without underwear! I'm outside the house for heaven's sake. You can't possibly expect me—" Kat was cut off by a stinging swat to her ass that caused her to quiet immediately. *Holy shit, I didn't even hear him move.*

"My instructions were quite clear, kitten. And yes, we will indeed expect you to as you so indelicately put it, 'run around without any underwear.' We'll expect to have unfettered access to what is ours—we'll want to be able to slide our fingers, tongues, or cocks into your sweet pussy whenever the urge strikes us. Panties will only be a barrier, and it will make us happy to know you're ready for our touch. Remember, your priority as our sub is to do what pleases us, just as our priority is to provide you with everything you need."

Okay, this was a side of Zach she hadn't seen before. She knew he was a Dom, but he'd always seemed like the more reasonable of the two brothers.

"Oh, kitten, you are so very easy to read. That's going to be very helpful in your training." Chuckling when her eyes widened in surprise, he continued, "You've always thought I'd be easier on you than Alex, am I close? Well, that isn't quite right. We are both going to be more than happy to push your boundaries. We'll listen to your questions and concerns, but ultimately, the decision about what happens during scenes and while you are in The Club or the bedroom will be ours. Now, remove your panties and hand them to me. I'll add this punishment to the others you've accumulated over the past ten days."

When she handed over the tiny triangle of material she thought was providing modesty, he lifted them to his nose and inhaled slowly. He enjoyed watching her pupils dilate and her cheeks flush.

"I love the way you smell, sweetness." Turning the little scrap of fabric inside out, he showed her the shine of her arousal. "I'd say someone is wet for me already. I think I'd like to check that up close." Kneeling in front of her, he said, "Spread your legs farther apart, kitten. I want to see just how aroused you have become from our discussion."

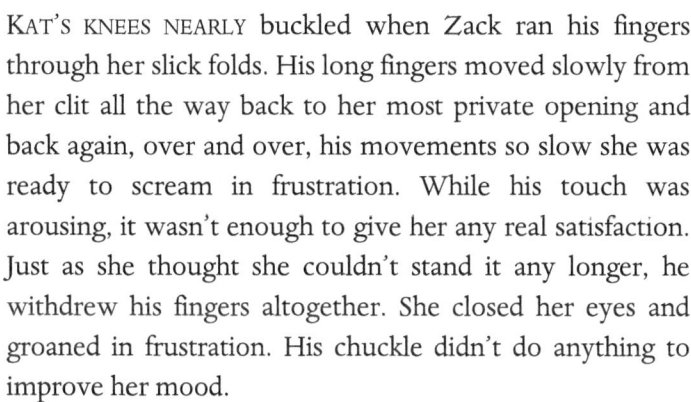

KAT'S KNEES NEARLY buckled when Zack ran his fingers through her slick folds. His long fingers moved slowly from her clit all the way back to her most private opening and back again, over and over, his movements so slow she was ready to scream in frustration. While his touch was arousing, it wasn't enough to give her any real satisfaction. Just as she thought she couldn't stand it any longer, he withdrew his fingers altogether. She closed her eyes and groaned in frustration. His chuckle didn't do anything to improve her mood.

"Patience, kitten. You'll have what you need, but all according to our schedule, not yours. I'm not done playing yet, and I think Alex would like to have a chance, too."

Kat's eyes flew open, and she looked over to see Alex leaning against a tree. Oh Lord, how long had he been standing there watching? It suddenly occurred to her if Alex could approach and watch without her hearing him, who else was out there? And that didn't even count the men monitoring the security system. *Oh God, there are people looking at me naked. I can't do this.*

ALEX WATCHED THE play of emotions move across Katarina's face at lightning speed. He was sure she was thinking about how she was being watched by people she couldn't see. He found it very interesting her reaction hadn't actually been fear, but more unease, followed by arousal.

She didn't seem quite sure how she should feel about it. Hmm. It seemed their little sub might be a bit of an exhibitionist. Well now, wasn't that going to be fun to explore? He gave her a bit longer to worry about exactly what he was going to do before slowly moving toward her.

"So, brother, catch me up. How has our beautiful woman done so far?"

"Well, she didn't follow the instructions she was given on how to dress. She was told to wear only a sundress and look what I found." Holding up her panties, Zach watched Alex look at Kat and raise one eyebrow in question.

"And the shoes?" Alex inquired.

"Well, I'd say she must not have trusted me to know she would be able to walk safely through the gardens barefooted because she chose to wear those as well. I'm sure we need to add punishments for both the panties and the shoes. How else will she learn to trust we would never put her in harm's way?"

Even though Alex knew Zach was trying to be stern, Kat couldn't have missed the note of teasing in his voice. Alex had to hold back his grin when she let out the breath she probably hadn't realized she'd been holding.

He was grateful she knew they weren't really angry with her. She needed to know they would never actually hurt her, but that didn't mean he didn't want her to be apprehensive about the whole punishment aspect of D/s relationship. The last time a Dom punished her, it had involved a single-tail whip and more pain than any sub should ever experience. His heart had nearly broken when she'd confided it was the worst pain she'd ever felt in her entire life. She'd said the lashes had been worse than being shot.

"Tell me what just went through your head, baby."

Alex stepped behind her, speaking over her shoulder. "Don't even think of editing it or lying, because I assure you, we'll know."

Kat stilled, she didn't even breathe for a few seconds. Alex could tell she was warring with herself on exactly how much she should reveal.

"Well, I–I was…"

Alex swatted her other ass cheek as he stepped around to face her.

"Stop thinking, Katarina. You're trying to figure out how to filter your answer. You are overthinking something that is really very simple. Just tell us *exactly* what you were thinking."

"Um, I was thinking how worried I am about punishments. I mean, I really don't know what you mean by that, and the last time a Dom said he was going to punish me, well, it didn't turn out so good."

Alex knew she'd deliberately left out being shot. Kat knew they both felt terribly guilty because they'd failed to protect her. Alex had taken it particularly hard, but as the oldest, it was his burden to bear.

"Go on. And remember, Katarina, I have already cautioned you against editing your response. Don't think I don't know you are holding back." Alex was not going to allow Kat to only reveal pieces of herself to them. They wanted it all. She'd learn just what all that entailed soon enough.

"Okay, well, damn… I was thinking the whip Cal used to punish me had hurt so much more that getting shot, and that makes me fear punishments even more."

Kat's answer was so softly spoken, he and Zach had barely been able to hear her. Neither of them responded for several seconds. Alex tried to mask the flash of pain that gripped him, but from the look on Kat's face, she hadn't missed it. Dammit, he's just inadvertently affirmed her instinct to hold back her deepest emotions. He could see the guilt in her eyes and had no one but himself to blame for putting it there.

"Thank you for telling us the truth, Katarina, I know it wasn't easy for you, and I'm sure I know why." Alex paused for several seconds before continuing. "The only way any Dominant and submissive relationship, let alone one that is a ménage, can work is if we're all completely open and honest with each other. There will be times when we don't think the other person wants to hear what we have to say and those will often be when it's most important to be completely transparent. You'll never be punished for being honest, baby. You will, however, be punished for lying. Lying is the one thing that absolutely will not be tolerated, and keep in mind, that includes lying by omission."

Alex felt certain Katarina wasn't thinking about the fact she was naked. She wouldn't realize speaking with her while she was fully exposed served more than one purpose. First, she'd become focused on the conversation and forgotten how ill at ease she'd initially felt without the artificial shield of her clothing. It also allowed both he and his brother to observe her body language, it was the perfect way to assess the honesty of her responses—it was nature's built-in lie detector. Additionally, being naked with them was something she needed to become accustomed to because they planned to keep her in various forms of undress when they were in The Club and in their home.

The sooner she became comfortable being exposed, the sooner they could move on to deeper aspects of the D/s lifestyle they planned to pursue. But none of those thoughts had any place in this afternoon's play. Alex and Zach had always felt any Dom worth his leathers knew even though you had to always plan ahead in a sub's training when in a scene, it was critical to keep your mind in the here and now. They always focused all their attention on the submissive in their care.

Chapter 21

"LET US EXPLAIN about punishments, kitten." Zach stood behind her and reached around her to cup her breasts. He rolled her nipples between his thumbs and forefingers, keeping a firm pressure on them as he gently pulled them into ever sharper peaks. "There are many forms of punishment, but always remember, we'll never physically harm you. That being said, punishment is not supposed to be fun, it's supposed to help you remember the lesson. When you forget a rule, ignore an order, or are disrespectful, you can expect a punishment that's intended to help you remember a more appropriate response the next time."

When Alex stepped up so close, he could feel the warmth of her body even though he was still fully dressed. When she started to raise her hands to touch him, he wrapped his fingers around her wrists and moved her hands back to her sides, holding them with a firm grip. Katarina's eyes widened, and her breathing sped up. *Perfect. Oh yes, little sub, so many tells. We are going to spend the rest of our lives learning each and every response.*

"Many Doms don't allow their subs to touch without permission, but Zach and I love your touch and will rarely institute that protocol. We enjoy the feel of your hands on us as much as we love touching you. We will always make sure you know when you're not allowed to touch without specific permission, you won't ever have to wonder.

"It's important you keep in mind not all Doms demand the same level of discipline, but we want you to be aware of all the things you may encounter when you're at The Club. We don't want you to be unpleasantly surprised or frightened by any of things you see or hear. Getting to know other members of The Club and talking to the other subs will help you learn as well. Don't ever think you're doing something wrong when they speak of things you haven't done. We are the only Doms you'll ever scene with, so if we haven't introduced it, you don't need to worry about it. We will, however, expect you to remain respectful and honest with any Dom you deal with, is that clear?" Alex knew they were giving her a lot of information at one time. It was a lot for new members to absorb, and even under the best of circumstances, it might be over-whelming.

Alex also knew that while he'd been speaking, he'd also been slowly drawing his fingers in slow circles over her lower abdomen, and his brother was still gently pinching her beautiful rose-colored nipples. Alex knew she would have trouble tracking the words when her body was being overwhelmed with sensation, and that's exactly as they'd intended. Beginning to program her body to crave their touch and to associate following their instructions with mind-numbing pleasure was a large part of what they wanted to accomplish, and judging by her soft sighs and low moans, she was finding quite a lot of pleasure in their touch. Katarina was absolutely stunning in her perfection. How he'd ever thought he could live without her was beyond his comprehension.

Alex picked up the conversation once again and added, "There are many types of punishments, from orgasm delay or denial to spankings, not to mention many 'specialty items' as we like to think of them. Neither my brother nor I are fans of whips as punishment. We're both well trained with whips and have found them helpful with subs who need a sharper edge of pain in order to find their release, so we are comfortable using them for pleasure enhancement, but that's not something we would be comfortable using with you now or perhaps ever."

Pausing briefly, Alex wanted to make sure she had a moment to process what he'd told her. He wanted to be sure she could put her fear of a single-tale out of her thoughts.

"We want you to use *red* as your safe word. It's also The Club's safe word, and it will be best if you only have to remember one. Subs sometimes forget their safe word or fail to use it when they should. We want you to always use yours if something is too much for you to endure, either physically or emotionally.

"When you say *red* everything stops immediately. We'll discuss what went wrong, and decisions about how to proceed will be made by the three of us together. If you're frightened and just need things to slow down, use the word *yellow*. That will tell us you're nearing your limit, and we need to reevaluate how things are going. We may or may not continue, but those decisions will be my brother's and mine."

Zach had not changed his touch at all while Alex was speaking to Kat, but knew their touch was arousing her, he could smell her essence from over her shoulder. As they'd planned, even combined, their intimate touches were not quite enough to give her the orgasm her body was craving.

Alex and Zach were also fully aware their little sub was getting mighty frustrated.

ALEX HAD MOVED her wrists together and held them easily with one hand at the small of her back while his other had moved into the curls at the apex of her thighs, his soft stokes just missing the spot where she most craved his touch. She was starting to fidget and was trying to move enough so his fingers would hit her clit. God, she was sure they were trying to slowly drive her insane. Neither one of them spoke for several seconds, and she was really getting annoyed with their teasing.

Finally, Alex broke the silence. "Be still, Katarina, we'll give you what you need when we are ready. Now, we made you an appointment with Clarissa, The Shadow-Dance Club's esthetician; we provide her with a small studio inside The Club and pay her membership fees. Many of our members appreciate not having everyone in our small town knowing about their woman's bare pussy. You'll hear her area referred to as The Spa by the other Doms and subs. I believe you'll enjoy your time there; Rissa, as she is known to her friends, is well liked by her clientele."

Swallowing the sudden lump in her throat, Kat squeaked. "You're going to let someone wax me? Down there? I don't know if I want to do that, it doesn't seem... well, I don't know, it just seems... wrong somehow."

Alex had moved his fingers to her wet center, and even though he'd felt Kat stiffen, she'd flooded his fingers despite her protests. Her words and responses weren't saying the same thing. *Ahh, love, your lovely body betrays you, yet again.* Pulling his now-soaked fingers through her wetness, Alex raised his fingers up in front of her, showing her just how aroused she'd become.

"Hmm, I think your body likes the idea, even when your mind is protesting. There will be many times we'll be giving you what you need even when it conflicts with what you think you want." When he'd finished speaking, Alex sucked the juices from his fingers, savoring the sweetness that was Katarina. "Oh, love, you taste so very sweet."

Kat wasn't sure her legs were going to continue to hold her upright. "Oh please… please, I need you to touch me." Kat didn't care it sounded like she was begging, she was just tired of all the talking, she needed more action. Good Lord, they'd reduced her thinking to some old country western song.

If they didn't do something about this soon, she was going to take matters into her own hands. She'd been taking care of her own pleasure for years, and she was so wound up now, it would only take her a few strokes to get herself off.

Her musing was cut short by Alex. "No, Katarina, having your pussy bare will please both Zach and me, we'll be able to see everything, and that will help us enhance your experiences. Also, you'll be pleasantly surprised by how much more sensitive you'll be. We're looking forward to feeling those smooth pussy lips against our mouths and sliding our cock heads over those swollen tissues as you become more and more aroused. Baby, your pussy just soaked my fingers, so don't tell me you aren't looking forward to that as well.

"Now, let's get your punishments out of the way so we can get to the pleasure we've all been looking forward to for this past week."

Chapter 22

A LEX KEPT SPEAKING to her as he took her hand and moved to a large, armless chair fashioned out of native rock she hadn't noticed just a few feet to the side of where they'd been standing. He sat down, but left her standing next to him.

"Katarina, Zach and I will always both be responsible for providing your punishments as well as your pleasure, and that is how we're going to begin today. Do you know why you are being punished, Katarina?" Alex's tone was blandly conversational, and that alarmed Kat for some reason.

Kat knew her breathing was getting faster by the minute, and she could almost feel her heart trying to beat itself right out of her chest. Damn, if she didn't slow herself down, she knew she was going to get light-headed. *Oh yeah, that'll go over great, pass out right here in front of them, naked no less. Sure, Kat, that'll really prove how ready you are for whatever they can dish out. Just because his voice evened out that doesn't mean you can lose your focus. Keep your head in the game. But... Cal's was just like this in the beginning, too.*

Kat's little self-talk had provided just enough hesitation that, from his position behind her, Zach gave her a stinging swat on the ass. Alex continued to watch her, saying, "Katarina, I asked you a question. Hesitation will not be

125

tolerated. Answer me now." His voice now held an edge, and she found comfort in the thought that at least he didn't seem so disinterested. She didn't trust disinterest anymore.

"Um… yeah, okay, well, I wore panties under my dress, oh and shoes, too." Kat knew her voice sounded small and airy. Hell, she was just grateful she hadn't sounded like Minnie Mouse on helium.

Alex raised one eyebrow at her. "And?"

"Well, I guess my spacing out when you asked me a question, but since Zach already swatted me, I'm thinking I've already been punished for that. So, I don't really know, and I'm really scared, and I don't know what else I've done wrong, I mean, I know I've made some really bad decisions, and you didn't seem very happy about me talking to Jenna when you didn't know we had reconnected and all, but that would probably be something you'd be more pissed at her about, so that must not be it, but then maybe because I was hiding up at the lake without your permission, I don't know if that's something I should really be punished for since it was before we, well, before we sorta got together, not that I think we're like a 'couple' or anything, shit, that's not really right either, um, I really, frack, I don't know, maybe because Jenna and I had those margaritas, but that can't be it, because you knew we were planning to do that, geez…"

Kat knew she was babbling, damn her runaway mouth. Thinking out loud as she preferred to view it, had gotten her into trouble more than a few times, but did she ever learn? Hell no. But it looked like Alex was working really hard to not smile, and she'd heard Zach's soft chuckle behind her, so maybe she wasn't in too much more trouble for not being able to figure out what else she'd done wrong.

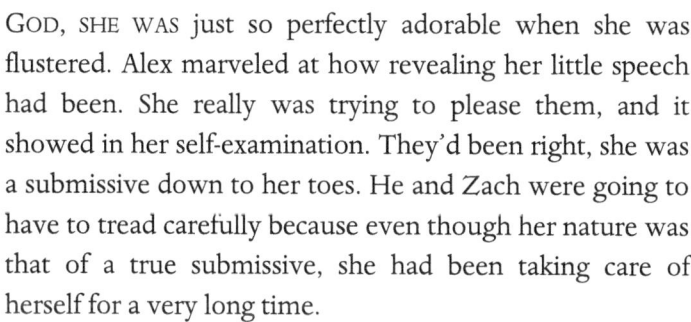

GOD, SHE WAS just so perfectly adorable when she was flustered. Alex marveled at how revealing her little speech had been. She really was trying to please them, and it showed in her self-examination. They'd been right, she was a submissive down to her toes. He and Zach were going to have to tread carefully because even though her nature was that of a true submissive, she had been taking care of herself for a very long time.

Further, she'd been raised by a single mother without ever having had a male authority figure in her life, so suddenly having two very dominant men to answer to was going to take some time and adjustment. Feeling like he would finally be able to speak without betraying his amusement at her little monologue, he finally continued.

"Well, let's review what's happened and which of those things Zach and I consider punishable offenses. First, you are correct about the panties and shoes, that's earned you five swats."

While Alex was talking to Kat, Zach had shifted her feet, so they were now shoulder width apart and began moving his fingers slowly through her damp heat. Looking over Kat's delicate shoulder, he smiled at his brother.

Alex knew by Zach's cheesy grin that Kat's pussy must have drenched Zach's fingers when he'd mentioned the five swats. Hell, the smell of her sweet honey was wrapping itself around him, making him wish this punishment was over and he could bury himself balls deep in her soaking pussy. He was relieved to know their little sub was more aroused by the thought of punishment than she was frightened—good to know.

"And, yes," Alex continued, "even though we knew you and Jenna were planning to make margaritas, we didn't know you planned to drink so much your decision-making skills would fly straight into the wind." With a smile he knew didn't reach his eyes, he added, "Allowing yourself to become so impaired you'd try to leave the suite against our direct orders you remain there has earned you five swats as well. Now, I also believe you mentioned us not wanting to sleep with you because of your scars." Alex had deliberately made sure his voice had become more menacing, and judging by Kat's wide-eyed look, she hadn't missed the change.

"Don't ever think we don't want you. You're also not allowed to devalue what belongs to us. Don't doubt for a minute that you are ours, Katarina. Your insult of what belongs to us will cost you an additional two swats. Now, I believe that totals twelve swats. I will begin, and then Zach will provide the last six. Since this is your first spanking, we won't require you to count them. Now, lie across my lap and let's get this over with."

KAT TOOK AN instinctive step back, only to hit the solid wall of Zach's chest. She was almost panting, she was breathing so hard. She was about two heartbeats away from total panic when Zach stepped around her and lifted her chin with the tip of his finger. Waiting until he knew her wide eyes had focused on him.

"Kitten, do you think we would ever truly harm you?" After Kat had slowly shaken her head from side to side, he continued. "What's your safe word, sweetness?"

"Um, it's red."

"Kat, I know you learned enough about our lifestyle to know how to properly answer a question during a scene. Want to try that again?" Zach still had his finger under her chin, her full focus on his face, his hold just enough that she'd feel the restriction; it was a small thing, but Zach knew it would help her slip more fully in to the proper mindset.

"It's red, Sir." Kat knew the words had been little more than a whisper, but he seemed satisfied with her answer. He nodded, then stepped back, taking her hand and gently pulling her forward so before she was fully aware of what he was doing, and she found herself laying over Alex's lap. In another instant, Alex had shifted her forward, so her ass was high in the air, and he'd moved her knees apart, completely exposing her pink pussy.

Oh God, she had never felt so vulnerable in her whole life, and the position was embarrassing beyond belief. Then she thought about the fact that there were cameras everywhere, and not only could other people have seen her naked, but now they'd be able to see everything. She began to twist and tried to get back up.

"Oh my God, the cameras, they'll be able to see me, you have to let me up, please, I don't think I can do this." She felt so ashamed, she knew her voice was cracking, she felt herself start to cry, and they hadn't even started spanking her yet.

ALEX REACTED QUICKLY or Kat would have twisted right off

his lap. She'd remembered the cameras sooner than he'd thought she would, but he should have known her mind was too sharp to be distracted so easily.

"Be still or you're going to earn yourself more swats, Katarina. You are not to worry about what anyone else can see, you are to put yourself in our care and trust we will always do what's in your best interest." She stopped trying to get back up, but he could feel her starting to hyperventilate; time to give her something else to think about.

THE FIRST SWAT was harder than Kat had expected, and she felt herself gasp in surprise. "Ow, damn it, that hurt!"

"Well, love, it wouldn't be much of a punishment if it didn't hurt, now would it?"

Kat wasn't too sure, but Alex sounded almost amused. Boy oh boy, if that didn't just about frost her cookies. If he thought she was going to let him beat on her and laugh about it, he was in for a mighty big surprise.

"Let me up, you can't hit me and then laugh about it, that's just, well, it's just mean." Kat was starting to get pissed now.

"First of all, we would never 'hit' you, this is a spanking, don't confuse the two. And I was not laughing at you, love. I was merely pointing out the obvious. Now, if you are quite through being a brat, let's begin *again*." And with that, he landed another swat on the other cheek. "One," Alex called out as he watched her ass blush beautifully. With each stroke, her cheeks turned a nice shade of pink.

As he continued to alternate his blows between her cheeks, her skin was becoming a deep pink, and he took a few seconds to hold his hand on her ass after each blow to make sure she'd feel the heat spread. He also took time to slide his fingers up and back through her slick folds.

"You're sopping wet, kitten. I think you're enjoying this more than you are willing to admit."

KAT FELT THE first stinging swats and bit down on her lip so she wouldn't cry out, but damn they hurt... they hurt a fucking lot. She'd promised herself she wasn't going to let them know how turned-on she was getting either. If they had any idea how her body was responding, they'd be wailing on her ass for every little infraction.

After the first two stokes, every time Alex's hand connected with her backside, it sent tiny jolts of electricity straight to her clit, and now, she was just hoping she could last through all their swats without coming. Holy shit, wouldn't *that* be embarrassing? Kat had been so lost in her musings, she was surprised when she heard Alex say, "Six."

"Now, kitten, stand up. Zach will give you the last half of your punishment, but before he does, we want to up the stakes a bit. Now lay over his lap while I make sure your pretty ass is ready for the plug we've brought along."

Before Kat could even respond, she found herself over Zach's lap with her legs spread even farther apart. She suddenly felt something cool being squirted on her back hole and she gasped. "Oh my God, what are you doing?"

"BE STILL, KITTEN, let Alex get you ready for the plug." Zach was holding her firmly around the waist, with his other arm over the back of her knees, so she couldn't move away from the cool gel Alex was dribbling over her pink rosette. God, he could hardly wait to fuck her there, but he knew it was going to take quite a lot of prep before she'd be ready. As Alex coated his finger and began rimming her, Zach felt her stiffen, and he tightened his hold in warning.

"Hold still, Katarina. Alex needs to get you lubed up, so he can push in the plug we bought for you. It's a small one. We'll need to stretch this beautiful little hole, so you can take us both at the same time. It won't happen today; we'll have to work you through a series of plugs in graduating sizes that will stretch you, so you'll be ready for us. Now, don't try to keep him out, relax, and push back into it."

He knew she was listening, or at least, she was probably trying. Her body's need was swamping her mind with endorphins, and Zach knew she was quickly becoming lost in the sensations being thrown at her. Her ass was a deep shade of rose, so it had to be burning already, and she was only halfway through her punishment.

The little nymph was already close to coming before Alex had finished the first six swats. Zach had almost laughed out loud at the look of relief on her face when Alex helped her to her feet, the short reprieve giving her a chance to bring herself back from the edge.

"How does it feel having his fingers pushing into your ass, kitten? I'll bet he could make you come just from playing with your pretty pink rear hole."

"Holy Mother of God, when his finger pushes so slowly inside… my whole body feels like it's going to explode."

Zach could feel her shaking, and from Alex's grin, he also knew how close she was. When she was on the very edge of release, Alex stopped moving. Kat groaned and tried to wiggle, but he held firm.

"Please, just a little more." Zach doubted she'd intended to say the words out loud because he'd felt her stiffen as they'd crossed her lips.

"Baby, did you think I wouldn't know you were about to orgasm? You won't be coming until we are ready for you to have your pleasure. Your orgasms belong to us, we'll be the only ones providing them. And we'll do so when we are ready, not just because you want one." Alex had started pushing the plug inside her, sliding it in just a bit before pulling it back out. Zach had heard subs describe the slow push and pull as *almost hypnotic* and the sexy sounds made him believe she was being pulled right into the vortex of sensation again.

GEEZ, WHAT WAS wrong with her? Kat didn't seem to be able to concentrate on anything because her body was a riot of conflicting feelings. She was sure she should be protesting Alex spanking her and now, shoving a butt plug the size of a damned fire hydrant up her ass. And speaking of her ass, it was currently sticking up like one of the local peaks, and her legs were far enough apart both men had now seen more of her then her damned doctor.

Yes indeed, she was pretty sure there was supposed to be a whole lot wrong with this situation, but she was having trouble figuring it out, her lust-fogged mind just didn't want to cooperate.

ZACH LOOKED UP and grinned at his brother; they could both tell Kat was slipping into subspace, that wonderful la-la land of lust that made a submissive feel like they were floating. Subspace produced boatloads of endorphins, and every submissive who'd ever reached that level of sexual submission described it as the ultimate happy place. Since they were trying to make sure Kat associated her submissive behavior and their touches with pleasure, this was the perfect outcome. The trick was going to be getting the plug in her ass and the rest of her swats taken care of before she went so deep, she wasn't cognizant of everything that was happening.

Alex finally seated the plug and stood back. Zach could see his brother was every bit as affected by what was happening as he was. *God, she is fucking amazing.* Zach started talking to her, needing to get her focus back quickly.

"Okay, kitten, let's get this punishment finished so we can fuck you and give you the orgasm we know you are craving. You took the first part of your punishment like a good girl, let's see if you can do as well under my hand." And with that he landed a solid slap to the center of her ass, just high enough she wouldn't feel the plug move; he was sure that would have been more than she'd have been able to take. He continued his swats, alternating cheeks and intensity and timing. Part of her arousal would depend on not being able to anticipate when the next blow would land or how long she'd have to wait.

When he only had one more swat to administer, he

heard her soft sniffle and knew she'd finally let go enough for the tears to start flowing. They'd known she would have barriers they would need to break down, and the fact that she was finally letting go of some of the tension she'd been harboring this last week was a sign they were making progress.

"Only one more, kitten. Are you ready?"

Kat's hiccupped "Y–yes, S–sir" brought a smile to his face. Even though he was convinced she was nearing her emotional and physical limit, she still remembered the response he'd had to prompt her to use earlier; she was everything he'd always known she'd be and more.

Zach landed the last swat squarely over the plug and at the same time said, "Come for us, kitten."

KAT FELT LIKE the world exploded all around her, surrounding her with swirling waves of brilliant color. Zach had told her to come at the same time he landed the last blow and her body reacted before his words had even fully registered. It seemed like forever, but she really didn't know how long she'd been lost in her own pleasure when she finally felt her breathing start to slow down a bit. She'd been able to feel her whole body shaking and was grateful Zach had kept a firm hold on her, or she was sure she'd have bounced herself right onto the rocks below his feet. Right now, all she could think about was how amazing it had felt to fly through all those colors.

She'd had orgasms before, well… if you counted what her little battery-operated boyfriend had given her as an orgasm, but this? Holy shit, this was something entirely different. Oh yeah, this confirmed their first experience together before she'd been shot hadn't been a fluke. The spanking hadn't even really hurt that much; as a matter of fact, she was pretty sure it had been arousing, but she needed to think about that and what it meant… later, yeah, she'd do that later… a lot later. Her brain didn't seem to be firing on all its cylinders right now, so she probably ought to shelve any attempts at thinking for right awhile.

Chapter 23

T HE INTENSITY OF her reaction to the spanking and plug probably shouldn't have surprised Alex as much as it had since he'd seen the depth of Katarina's submissive nature. But her instantaneous response to his brother's order to come had certainly blindsided him. In all the years Alex had been a sexual dominant, he'd never met a woman who was a more natural-born sexual submissive. Hell, he'd known submissives who'd been living the lifestyle for years who didn't go into subspace that easily, nor did they react as explosively as she had. He'd nearly come himself just watching her.

Zach sat her up as soon as they were convinced she'd started coming back down from her orgasm, and they both smiled at the dazed look on her flushed face. She still wasn't completely back in the here and now, and it was the sexiest thing he'd ever seen. Alex handed Zach one of the soft subbie blankets they kept in nearby hidden bins, then stood close as his brother wrapped it securely around Kat's soft shoulders.

The Club had strict rules emphasizing aftercare for subs for many reasons. The importance of those few moments of cuddle time after a scene was continually stressed in all their training classes. The small gestures of consideration—the sips of cool water, the small bites of a favorite treat—were critical to not only a sub's bonding experience with her Dom, but the extra time also gave the submissive a chance to regain his or her emotional footing.

Zach would provide some of Kat's aftercare, then he'd place Katarina into Alex's waiting arms. They would both enjoy these tender moments as much as she would, he was sure of that. Even though his cock was screaming to be buried as deep inside Kat as he could get, making her feel cherished was much more important.

Kat heard Zach softly say, "You handled that beautifully, kitten. I'm very proud of you." Then he kissed her softly on the end of her nose and moved her onto Alex's lap.

ALEX GAZED AT Katarina's face, her cheeks still flushed, and her eyes still didn't seem to be fully focusing. She'd managed a smile at the words of praise Zach had spoken to her before his brother had moved her gently into his care, and Alex knew he'd lost his soul to her in that moment. He'd always known he loved her, but this was something so much deeper. This was a soul-deep connection beyond anything he had words to describe. Despite hearing his father and other friends describe their feelings when they connected with 'the one' he'd been totally unprepared for the surge of emotion he was experiencing.

Possessiveness, passion, longing, lust, and some things—he was sure language hadn't evolved enough to even label yet—inside his chest and came to rest over his heart. Christ, if his team could hear these thoughts, they'd think he was the biggest sap who had ever lived, but right now, he wasn't even sure he'd mind their teasing.

Alex knew the minute Katarina's analytical mind kicked back into gear. Her muscles tensed, and he could almost feel the embarrassment coming off her in waves. Moving to stand her on her feet, Alex said, "Well done, love. But now, we're going to fuck you right out here in the gardens, because, baby, I for one can't wait to get my cock inside your tight sheath. You'll be even tighter with that plug in your ass." Kat's mouth dropped open, but Alex didn't give her a chance to speak before he continued.

"Oh yes, love, I'm going to slide my cock into your warm, lush heat, and you're going to feel every bump and ridge pressed against the front of your pussy. And while I'm pumping into your pussy, you're going to give Zach some relief with that beautiful mouth. He's going to be sliding between your lush lips and losing himself in heaven. Have you ever given a man a blow job, baby?"

It seemed to take Kat a couple of seconds to realize Alex had actually asked her a question. Damn, he loved watching the way she responded to his voice; it was almost as if he could cast a spell over her with words. It wouldn't be long before she would be able to identify the mood of the scene by the voice they used.

"Um, yeah, but I wasn't good at it, I guess," Kat finally managed to answer.

Alex tilted his head slightly to the side and asked her, "Why would think you weren't any good at it, baby?"

"Well, Cal made me do it once, and he kept having one of his men hit me with a thick paddle because he said I wasn't doing it right. He said it was the only way for me to learn." Kat's voice had almost faded completely away by the time she'd finished speaking. She lowered her head, trying to hide that her eyes had filled with tears.

Kat was sure this had to be one the most humiliating

moments of her life; if she'd failed to please a wannabe Dom like Cal, two experienced Doms like the Alex and Zach Lamont were sure to be disappointed. Wishing she could just disappear, she couldn't bear to look up and see the disillusionment she was sure she would find in their expressions.

ALEX WAS SO angry, he knew he had to get himself under control before speaking to Katarina. When he looked up, he knew his brother was feeling the same way. If he ever got close enough to Cal Robertson, he was going to kill the bastard with his bare hands. Rebuilding Katarina's fragile self-esteem was going to have to take precedence over some of the other things they'd planned for her. He'd been looking forward to her training, but her emotional well-being was their responsibility, and this was clearly something she was struggling with.

Using his forefinger, Alex gently raised her face to his and was nearly undone by her tear-filled sea-blue eyes. "Katarina, don't believe anything that bastard said to you. We'll be happy to help you with anything you're unsure about. I promise you, when you wrap those sweet lips around our cocks, everything you do is going to be right. I know I can tell you this all afternoon long and likely, you are going to still feel unsure. You're worried about disappointing us, aren't you?"

Kat looked stunned he'd seen through her emotions so clearly, and all she managed was a slow nod of her head, causing a tear to spill over and trail down her cheek. Alex leaned forward and kissed the salty drop away. "Let us show you just how wonderful we can be together." And with that, he helped her stand and watched as her pupils dilated when she noticed that Zach standing in front of her, stark naked.

Alex stepped behind Kat and pulled her back against his chest, wrapping his arms around her tightly before taking first one step and then another back until he was once again sitting on the rock chair. Spreading her lets apart, Alex ran his fingers through her wet folds to be sure she was ready to take him inside her sweet pussy.

"Step back, love. That's right, straddle my legs so I can enter you from behind—you're going to love this angle. Now slowly lower yourself onto my cock. When I'm fully seated inside you, you'll be able to lean forward and take Zach's cock into your mouth."

KAT GLORIED IN Alex and Zach's pure male perfection. They were tall and muscular, and their skin always looked like they'd just returned from an island adventure... she loved their golden tan complexion. Their broad shoulders and thick chests topped long, thick cocks. The whole package was a sight to behold. Oh yeah, she could just look at them for hours. When she realized she'd been staring, she looked up to see Zach grinning at her.

"Like what you see, kitten?" Even though his tone was teasing, his lust-filled eyes told her just how pleased he'd been by her consideration. "Come here, sweetness."

As she slid down onto Alex's rigid length, she didn't even try to hold back her moan. Leaning toward Zach, she felt his fingers thread through her hair in a slow move that was pure seduction. He smiled, his focus on her breasts and Kat felt her nipples peak in response to his gaze.

"You are so very beautiful, inside and out, we are the luckiest men in the world."

Kat loved how patient they were with her, they took the time to explain what they were going to do, and that helped lessen her apprehension. When she'd started lowering herself onto Alex, the engorged head of his cock parted her slick folds, and she heard his quiet hiss. She bit her lip to suppress a smile of satisfaction knowing she could draw that reaction from him. Alex's hands on her hips tightened, and he slowed her descent.

"Slow down, baby, I want to enjoy my slide into heaven and give your swollen tissues a chance to stretch around me. Oh, sweet Mother of God, you feel amazing. The plug in your ass makes you even tighter than before, and it's the sweetest torture in the world. We're going to have to go carefully, or I'll never last. Holy fucking hell, you're already rippling and pulsing around me. It feels like my cock is being squeezed inside a wet velvet glove. Fucking amazing."

When she'd finally lowered herself all the way down on Alex's cock, Kat leaned forward as Zach shuffled closer to her. He was standing back enough to slowly stroke up and back down the length of his cock with one hand and the other tightened in her hair. His gaze was focused on watching her pussy lips wrapping around his brother's cock as she slowly sank down and took Alex inside her.

Kat reached out and took Zach's cock into her hand, running her fingers over the smooth skin, marveling at the feel of velvet soft skin wrapped over heated steel. She wasn't surprised when she couldn't get her hand wrapped all the way around his girth. Using her fingertips to trace every bump, ridge, and vein, she noticed the pearly drop beaded on the tip, and ran her tongue along the moist slit to get her first taste of him. Zach's sharply inhalation had her looking up into his eyes and smiling.

"Will you tell me what you like? I want to learn how to please you both."

ZACH KEPT HIS gaze locked on her face, his expression tight. God, it was taking a Herculean effort to not plunder her sweet mouth. Taking a slow breath, Zach spoke quietly.

"Kitten, you'll always please us, just do what feels natural to you, and I'll guide you on details, but right now, my body is yours to explore. Alex and I are also enjoying learning all the little spots that light you up. Take your time to touch and taste me."

Kat continued to run her soft hands all over his engorged cock, and the visual contrast between her pale fingers and his naturally bronzed skin was arousing by itself, but her mouth? Sweet baby Jesus, he was employing every trick he knew to delay the orgasm already tingling up and down his spine, boiling just below the surface. He hadn't come in a woman's hand since he'd been a teenager, and he was praying he wouldn't embarrass himself now.

Kat licked her lips just before she slid them around the mushroom-shaped head and began to take Zach to the back of her throat. When she triggered her gag reflex, Zach whispered, "Breath through your nose, kitten, it will help you avoid gagging, but please remember, taking a cock to the back of your throat is a learned skill. You'll get it, take your time, this isn't a race." With his words of encouragement, Zach could see the muscles in her shoulders relax; looking up at his brother, Zach saw Alex's knowing look.

ALEX GRIPPED KATARINA'S hips and began to slowly lift her before lowering her back onto his length. He wanted to build up slowly, knowing it was going to take concentration on both his and Zach's part to be sure they all came at the same time. He could tell by the look on his brother's face that Kat's oral skills were quickly moving him to the point of no return.

"Oh my God, Alex, our woman is a natural with her sweet mouth. She's taking me in farther with each stroke, and when she seals those sweet lips around me…" Zach sounded like he was getting close. "Kitten, if you don't want to swallow, you need to let go, now!"

Zach felt her throat muscles working and her jaw clench as she sucked harder and moved him deeper in her throat. It was obvious she wasn't going to shy away from letting him fill her mouth with his seed. "Alex, I'm not gonna last, push her over right now. Oh fuck, kitten, holy shit, your mouth is pure magic."

Alex was holding Kat and pumping into her with short, sharp stokes, then he reached around, pinched her clit, and said, "Katarina, come now" just as he saw his brother stiffen, knowing he was pulsing into her mouth. Alex felt like an electric shock had rocketed down his spine, squeezing and setting fire to his balls, never had he come so suddenly or so fiercely. He knew Katarina had come immediately at his command, her passion and responsiveness as close to perfect as he'd ever seen in any submissive.

Adding that to the fact she was theirs made him realize he would need to spend every day thanking the powers above for the treasure that was their sweet Katarina.

Chapter 24

L YING OUT NEXT to the pool, enjoying what was likely one of the last days of summer, Kat was floating in that foggy place between sleep and wakefulness when she heard a woman's rapid chatter coming from inside the house. Selita's excited words slowly started to soak through the haze... *telephone... visitor... biggest client... Miss McKay...* Okay, now Selita had Kat's attention.

Bringing herself upright, Kat started to pull on the shirt she'd borrowed from Zach before making her way to the pool. Sure, Alex and Zach had bought her beautiful new clothing, including a sheer lace beach cover-up, but she preferred to wrap herself in something that smelled like one of them, and they never seemed to tire of seeing her in one their shirts, particularly when they knew she wasn't wearing anything underneath it.

As Kat entered the house, she heard Selita's agitated voice as she spoke rapidly to Alex. "He act like I don't know Katarina's name, calling her Miss McKay. He treat me like a common servant, he does not know that I'm a part of this family. He talked like he a big shot, trying to put the sheep over my face, I say you. He tell me to 'convey' a message to Miss McKay that her biggest client will be paying her a visit soon, he too large for his branches if you asking me."

Kat's brain fog let her spiral into her memories as she thought back on all the times she and Jenna had laughed at the way Selita could mess up American slang and expressions. They long ago decided it was far more entertaining to just listen than try to figure out what expression she was butchering. Even if they'd ever been able to get a word in, where would be the fun in correcting her?? Realizing she hadn't really been listening, Kat started to focus and suddenly realized Selita had said the caller claimed he was her biggest client.

"I tell him to wait on the line, and I bring Katarina inside to take his call, but he say, 'No, just be sure you give her the message,' and he still won't say his name. I'm sorry, Alex, I called you from your office right away, because it just do not seem so right to me."

Alex assured Selita she'd indeed done exactly the right thing, then he turned to Katarina as she stood in the doorway listening.

"Who was your largest client, love?" Kat knew by the expression on Alex's face he'd seen all the blood drain from her face. Alex Lamont was no one's fool, he'd known Cal Robertson had made that phone call. Alex moved quickly to wrap his arm around her shoulder and lead her to a chair in front of the fireplace. He sat beside her and brushed her long blonde curls back over her shoulder and waited patiently until she looked up at this face. "Katarina, tell me who made that call."

"Cal," was all Kat was able to say around the lump in her throat. There hadn't been any incidents in so long, she'd hoped he'd found another obsession, and she'd be able to get her life back. In a soft whisper, she added, "Why would he want to come here? Why me? Why does he want me? Why warn me? I don't understand."

If Alex hadn't been watching her, he wasn't sure he would have even heard the litany of questions. The abject fear in her small voice made him see red. How dare that bastard frighten Katarina in her own home. This was the one place she should always feel safe. This was the second time her security had been shattered while in his care, and he was getting damned tired of it.

Her eyes were hazy and unfocused with fear, but she watched him with a steady regard as he reached for his phone. He alerted Zach and their security team; and in less than a minute the room began filling with men. Alex hated the catatonic look in Kat's eyes. She looked numb, and that was the last thing a passionate woman like Katarina should ever feel.

"I can't believe it's happening again. Will I ever be free of this nightmare? I've set a new record for screwing up and it's truly humbling."

Alex knew she'd been thinking aloud and even though he appreciated the insight, her words broke his heart. As the security staff started discussing strategy and possible scenarios, Kat appeared to be trying to make herself as small and invisible as possible.

Zach had taken their best marksmen, Ethan Jantz and James Creed, out to scout locations overlooking various access roads to the house. Both men had returned stateside recently, and after deciding they'd had enough of Uncle Sam's 'See the World' travel itinerary, had joined their former teammates at ShadowDance. Ethan and James were probably the best snipers the U.S. Special Forces had seen in a generation, and Alex was grateful those considerable skills would be focused on protecting Katarina.

Alex had moved away from her side and was deep in discussions with Colt and Grayson when he looked over to see Katarina sitting in the very corner of the sofa with her legs pulled up to her chest, her arms wrapped tightly around her knees, her little bare toes curled under her feet. Excusing himself, he moved to her side.

"Are you all right, love?" When Alex saw how pale she was, he knew she was close to crashing despite her slow nod. "Well, let's get you upstairs and into a nice warm bubble bath, shall we?" Alex knew his brother and their entire security staff were all working to make sure she remained safe, and right now his first responsibility was to care for the emotionally fragile woman who held his heart in the palm of her hand. Easing her into his arms, he stood, nodded to Colt as he walked out of the room, and headed up the stairs. He'd make sure she was properly pampered and resting before returning to his office, and until then, Alex knew Zach and Colt were more than capable of managing all the details.

KAT FELT AS if she'd fallen through Alice's looking glass, it was as if she could see everything happening around her, but all the sounds were muted, and the colors surrounding her were dull. She remembered Alex inquiring about how she was doing; her slow nod hadn't convinced him she was all right. If she was honest with herself, she wasn't sure she would ever be okay again.

Perhaps if she could just disappear, then Cal would give up and leave all the people she cared about alone. She felt terribly guilty for having brought all this trouble to door of the people who'd always treated her like family. If anything happened to any of the Lamonts, Selita, or their friends, she wasn't sure she'd ever be able to forgive herself.

After Alex helped her out of the warm bubble bath she'd soaked in, he gently dried her and carried her to bed. He stayed beside her until he thought she'd fallen asleep, and then he softly kissed her forehead before slipping from the bed. Before he left the room, she heard him remove the pistol they'd spent so many hours insisting she learn how to handle from the nightstand drawer. He set it on the nightstand where she could reach it easily. It had become a nightly ritual—they'd made sure she put the gun within reach every night before retiring to their own rooms.

They still didn't sleep through the night in the suite with her, insisting they would do so when she was ready to make a permanent commitment to the relationship. Kat knew there would never be any other man in her life. She had loved both Alex and Zach since she'd been little more than a young girl, but she also knew she'd made some pretty significant mistakes recently. She'd asked for a little time, so they could all be sure what they wanted. She had planned to tell them she was ready this coming weekend. They were planning to finally take her to The Club, and she'd wanted to surprise them with her decision that evening.

Now, as Kat lay awake looking out the French doors that led to the wraparound deck outside the suite, she weighed the pros and cons of staying versus slipping into the night to protect the people who'd been the closest thing to an extended family she'd ever known. Tears blurred her vision as she saw everything she'd ever wanted slipping through her fingers, and her weekend plans evaporated into a fine mist. She was going to have to walk away from Alex and Zach, yet again.

It seemed like fate was working against her ever getting to go to The Club, and that just plain pissed her off. Even though they'd taken her through while the cleaning crews had been working, she'd yet to see any of the equipment in use or gotten to feel the surge of energy which always surrounded people becoming one with the music, losing themselves as they danced and abandoned their inhibitions in kink. Sighing, Kat rolled back over when she thought she heard a floorboard creak and found herself looking up into the very angry face of Cal Robertson.

Chapter 25

"**N**OT ONE SOUND, bitch."

Cal's voice sent shards of ice through Kat's veins. She was frozen in place, too afraid to do anything but breathe. She knew either Alex or Zach would be in to check on her any minute, they wouldn't leave her alone for long, not with the threat she'd received and how poorly she'd responded. If she could just reach the gun, she'd shoot the bastard herself. Even though she'd never considered herself a violent person, she would gladly kill him before she let him hurt her men. Cal spoke to her in the same arrogant, condescending tone he'd used that last night, the night he'd whipped her to within an inch of consciousness.

"You didn't really think you could get away from me, did you, Kat? That I wouldn't find you and finish what I'd started? And now, you've been letting two strangers fuck you, what a slut you've become, my disobedient little slave. I own you, Kat, don't ever forget that, you don't eat or drink without my permission. Fuck, you don't even breathe unless I allow it. I warned you repeatedly. You are mine."

Cal was slowly moving closer to the enormous bed. God in heaven, she was grateful for its ridiculously large size because the time it took him to come closer to her bought her some time to think. With each step he took toward her, Kat instinctively moved an equal distance away. She hoped Cal wouldn't realize he was pushing her closer to the pistol.

"Stop moving away from me. You should know better than trying to avoid my hand. I'll be punishing you for escaping from the club in Vegas and for opening those beautiful thighs for someone other than me."

As he stepped closer, she could smell the liquor on his breath. Even though they hadn't spent a lot of time together, it had been easy to see Cal was a mean drunk. Hell, he was mean when he was sober, and when he started drinking, he became almost demonic. Kat had seen him burn the forearms of employees with red-tipped cigars because they delivered a drink or meal too slowly.

One night when she'd been headed down the stairs in his mansion, she'd watched from the shadows in horror as he'd sliced open the throat of a man who'd worked for him for over a decade as the man's horrified wife looked on… the man's crime? He'd delayed making a delivery, so he could attend his young daughter's piano recital. After the man crumpled in a heap to the floor, Cal had handed the wife off to his staff for their entertainment.

Kat had already known she was in over her head, but that night had shown her that risking escape was the only choice she had. She'd slipped back upstairs to the guest suite and stayed out of sight until the next morning. Cal had sensed the change in her and refused to let her out of his sight. He'd taken her to his favorite dungeon club that very night. She was sure he had planned to kill her during the scene, and the opportunity she'd had to get away from him had been pure providence. As he stood in front of her now, telling her in excruciating detail all the ways he was going to hurt her, she didn't doubt for a single second he would follow through.

"If you call out to your new fuck buddies, I'll take great pleasure in killing them both while you watch. And I'll kill anyone who comes after you after I've taken you away from this God-awful place. Honestly, Kat, a ranch? How very hillbilly of you. I was willing to give you everything, all you had to do was cooperate and keep your mouth shut. But no, you had to make me out a fool by escaping in the middle of our evening at the club, didn't you? Just a short bathroom break, you begged. Then you slipped out through the night.

"I know who helped you, you know, and she paid dearly for that transgression. I hear she's recovering at the University Hospital, and when she's healed, I'll find her again. No one disrespects me without eventually paying for it with their life, something you'd do well to remember, you worthless cunt."

Kat saw him raise his hand, but didn't register his movement before pain exploded in her head as fire seared the side of her face. She landed on her hands and knees on the floor in front of the nightstand, having been spun to face the opposite direction by his blow. It took a few seconds for her to realize she'd been hit so hard, she'd actually been knocked off the bed.

"Get up, you stupid whore, we're leaving now."

Kat knew she would only have one chance. As she gingerly used the nightstand to bring herself upright, she palmed the pistol. With her head swimming, she managed to turn completely around before he had time to walk around the large four-poster bed. Without hesitating, she flicked the safety off, raised the gun, and fired straight at Cal's chest just as the door to the suite burst open.

It seemed like the entire world went into slow motion. Katarina heard the deafening retort of the gun, watched Cal's eyes widen as red blossomed over his chest, and he sank slowly to his knees. At the same time, Alex and Zach burst into the room, Zach catching her as her knees folded out from under her.

ALEX AND ZACH'S office was located directly under Katarina's suite, and when they heard the sound of something hitting the floor, they raced up the stairs and down the hall as if the hounds of hell were on their heels.

Call it instinct, but they knew Kat was in trouble. Just as they reached for the ornate handles on the double doors, the sound of a single gunshot sounded from the other side, and Zach was sure his heart had stopped beating until they saw Cal Robertson sinking to the floor and Katarina holding the small pistol he'd left on the table clutched in her shaking hands. Zach was a step ahead of Alex, reaching her just as she collapsed.

Zach inhaled deeply as soon as he had Kat wrapped safely in his arms. He was sure he'd stopped breathing somewhere near the top of the stairs, he'd been in such a panic to reach her. He'd had years of military training and spent most of his years in the service doing black ops in places the devil wouldn't spend time, but this, without question, had been the most frightening moment of his life.

When he'd heard that loud thump come from Kat's suite, he'd felt his blood run cold, and the sound of a gun firing before they could reach her took at least a decade off his life. Zach let the others secure the scene and work on

Robertson. Personally, he didn't think anyone was going to make much effort to save his sorry ass, and that was fine with Zach. The only person he was concerned with was the beautiful, brave woman he was holding cradled in his arms.

ALEX WATCHED AS Zach scooped Katarina up and moved down the hall within seconds, so she wouldn't have to be a part of the chaos which had erupted yet again in a place that was supposed to be her sanctuary. He and Zach had spent most of last night discussing how they were going to convince Katarina to marry them. Even if they had to beg on their hands and knees, they weren't willing to wait any longer.

They'd already started planning an extended honeymoon, and now they'd be adding a complete remodel to the suite while they were gone. Alex wanted to make sure she wasn't haunted by any ghosts of her past trauma. When they returned, both he and Zach would move into the suite with her, and the three of them would begin building the family they'd heard her tell Jenna she longed for so many years ago.

Alex still remembered standing in the back of the barn with Zach, listening to their younger sister and her best friend talking about their respective futures. Jenna's had been full of travel, career goals, and far-flung adventures. Katarina's dream was to have a houseful of children to love and a man who loved her as much as she knew she would love him. He knew neither he nor his brother had forgotten that night, and now, they were both committed to doing everything in their power to make certain her dream came true.

SEVERAL HOURS LATER, Cal Robertson's body had been removed from their home, and the last of Dylan Marshall's questions had finally been answered. Alex and Zach had called in a cleaning service to restore order to her suite, and they'd finally left a few minutes earlier.

Kat knew it was important to go back to the suite tonight. If she didn't face it right away, it would be even more difficult tomorrow night. She had never considered herself a person who backed away from something that frightened her... *Oh, my God, that's exactly what I've been doing by not telling Alex and Zach how I feel about them. That everything I've ever wanted... every dream I've ever had is right here at ShadowDance. What a coward I've been, well, no more...*

"Penny for your thoughts, love." Kat hadn't heard Alex move into the room. Zach had taken her downstairs into the relative quiet of their office, and Selita had brought her cold compresses for her rapidly swelling face. God, she was going to have one hell of a shiner by tomorrow morning. Zach hadn't gone ten seconds without touching her as if he was afraid she'd disappear if he let go of her for more than a moment.

"Oh, Alex, I'm so glad you're here." Kat launched herself off the sofa and into his arms.

THE LOVE ALEX felt at that moment overwhelmed him. Feeling as if his chest might burst with it, all he could do was hold her tightly against him and breathe in the unique scent of citrus shampoo and sweet woman that was always their Katarina. She wrapped her legs around his waist and clung to him, and he felt her warm tears soaking his neck as her body heaved with sobs so gut-wrenching, he worried she was going to make herself sick.

"Katarina, talk to me, baby. Are you all right?" Alex could hear the concern in his own voice, but he wasn't sure Kat had heard him over her hiccupping sobs. Alex sat down with her on his lap facing Zach who was looking on with an equally concerned expression.

"I am now that you're both here. I was so frightened. I was afraid he was going to hurt you. I knew I'd only have one chance, and I was so far from the gun, but when he knocked me off the bed, I landed right in front of where you'd left it for me on the nightstand. He thought he'd hurt me, but really, he'd put me right where I needed to be.

"When I turned around, all I could think about was I had to make sure he didn't hurt you or anyone else. I remembered everything Colt said when he was teaching me to shoot and did just what he said. I just pointed the gun at the middle of his chest and pulled the trigger. I didn't even stop to think about how I was hurting someone else, because protecting the men I love is more important than anything else, and I know I'm babbling again. I'm sorry. I can't help it. And I have to tell you both right now, I didn't want to tell you separately because I know that isn't how you said we had to do it if we wanted to make this work, but now you're here, and I want you to know that you and Zach are everything I've ever dreamed of, I love you both so much, and if you both still want to marry me, I want that more than anything else in the entire world."

Kat sagged against Alex's chest; he marveled at how she'd been able to say all that while seemingly not taking a single breath and let the joy of her words soak in.

When Alex finally released her, Zach shot to his feet, and pulled her into his embrace. "Oh, kitten, you have just made us the happiest men in the world. Of course, we still want to marry you. Tomorrow wouldn't be too soon for us, but we want you to have the wedding of your dreams."

Alex chuckled, and added, "Absolutely, anything your heart desires, it's yours, but you'd better start planning quickly, love, because you have one month from this moment to make it happen or we'll kidnap you and elope which will get us all in buckets of trouble with Mama Catherine. First thing tomorrow, we'll begin sharing our joyous news, but for tonight, I believe we have a fiancé who needs some decoration. What do you think brother?"

Zach moved quickly to the safe, reaching inside, returning with the ring they'd help design and had specially made for Kat the minute she'd re-entered their lives. Alex held her hand steady as Zach slid the platinum and diamond creation onto her delicate finger. The band was narrow with scrolled etchings holding sapphires, highlighting a huge princess-cut diamond that sparkled under the light. Zach had to swallow around the lump of emotion that had formed in his throat at the sight of their ring on her finger.

"The sapphires reminded us of your beautiful blue eyes, kitten. And we know they're also your birthstone."

"Oh, Zach, Alex, it's the most beautiful ring I've ever seen. I can't believe you had it already. I'm the luckiest woman I know." Kat's tears started to fall again, but these were tears of happiness.

"Katarina, we commissioned that ring the morning after we found you at the lake. We knew then we'd never let you go. You are ours, you've always belonged to us, even when we didn't know it." Alex's voice had begun to crack with emotion, but he didn't care. It was important for his future wife to know just how important she would always be to them.

Chapter 26

Three Months Later

KAT COULDN'T BELIEVE Alex and Zach were finally going to take her to The Club. It seemed like she'd waited forever for this night. They promised her they were planning to introduce her to a few Club members at a small gathering out on the terrace before everyone actually went into The ShadowDance Club itself. They insisted it would give her a chance to meet a few of the other submissives ahead of time, so she would be able to talk to them and ask questions openly. Both men wanted her to feel comfortable once they were inside and 'the rules' applied. Holy shit, there were so many rules, Kat's head had been reeling for few weeks as they'd taught her all the expectations and Club etiquette.

They'd given her a month to plan the wedding of her dreams, and with their mother's help, they'd managed it a scant two days before the deadline. Kat still maintained having the gardens, which were the most picturesque place she knew, outside their backdoor had been the only reason they'd been able to pull it together so quickly. Of course, once you added in the steamroller that was her new mother-in-law, Catherine Lamont, to the mix, things seemed to go much smoother. People always seemed to be able to accomplish monumental feats after a single call from Catherine. Laughing to herself, Kat remembered the flowers she'd been assured couldn't be delivered in time, arriving after a discreet call placed by Catherine.

Standing at the back windows, looking out as the fading sunlight danced over the gardens, Kat thought back to their wedding day. The legal ceremony itself had taken place that morning at the small city hall in town. The local justice of the peace, who also ran the hardware store, had married Alex and Katarina with a few quick words only witnessed by Zach, Jenna, and their parents. Legally, Kat could only marry one of the brothers, and since Alex was two whole minutes older, he was now her 'paper husband' as she liked to tease him. But the joining ceremony that evening in the gardens was the ceremony which had joined her heart to both brothers, and the one that mattered to her. *It* was the wedding she'd always remember.

Catherine had managed to have a bridge with a center gazebo built over the natural rock-lined pool. Kat had felt like a princess as she'd walked across the bridge toward her two grooms. Catherine had insisted it was a symbolic *crossing over* into a new life, and Kat had to admit, she had felt every bit of that change clear down to the deepest parts of her soul as she'd made her way to them.

The foliage surrounding the pool area had been strewn with thousands of tiny lights, and the subtle underwater lights added a surreal glow. The whole evening had been completely enchanting. She would never forget her fairy-tale wedding and having gained her best friend as a sister-in-law was the sweet icing on the cake.

She and her husbands had danced the night away before leaving the next morning on a month-long honeymoon which had taken them to too many of the world's most famous beaches to count. Kat had snorkeled in places she'd only seen on the Travel Channel or read about in magazines. The white sands of the Philippines had been a favorite of hers. All their travels as soldiers had made the men harder to impress, but they'd insisted they were seeing it all again for the first time through her eyes, proving her two Doms could be as romantic as they were demanding.

Her husbands had packed for her, remembering everything she'd needed for their trip except her birth control pills. She was still undecided about whether or not she believed that had actually been an accident. She didn't really care, she wanted nothing more than to fill their home with children, so she had decided to not worry about whether or not she'd been 'had', literally.

The first night on the plane Alex had explained in detail how they had planned to continue stretching her so she would be able to take them at the same time. She knew her face had paled; her limited experience with anal play before Alex and Zach had been terrifying. But true to his word, they had spent days prepping her, stretching the sensitive tissues, so she could enjoy their double penetration. The series of plugs they'd bought her made the one they'd used in the gardens look miniscule.

On the final night of their trip, they'd led her out to a secluded beach for dinner. They'd had a beautiful tent set up, and the whole thing had reminded her of a sinful hideaway for a desert sheik. The food had been some of the best she'd ever tasted, and the torches used for lighting had added to the ambiance. Their attention to romantic detail always made her feel cherished and special.

Once they'd all finished eating, Alex and Zach had demanded she strip and dance for them before they tied her between two posts and flogged her until her skin had become so sensitized, she would have sworn they'd electrified every square inch. When they finally moved her to the enormous pillows at the back of the huge tent, she'd been so desperate for them, she'd nearly been blinded by need.

Zach had laid down and positioned her, so she was straddling him, and his rock-hard length slid between her wet folds. When she'd tried to impale herself on him in one swift move, he'd given her several stinging swats which had only served to send her so close to orgasm, it had taken every ounce of her fragile control to hold back the release she didn't have permission to take. Even now, every time she thought about that night, she could feel her pussy flood with her sweet cream.

Alex had taken great care to make sure she was adequately prepared for him. His fingers massaged so much lube into her tight hole, she'd sworn she ought to be able to taste it. She would never forget the soft words he'd spoken to her just before he'd breached her ass with his cock.

"Now, my love, you will be ours in every way. We are going to mark you in a way that you have yet to even imagine. And bring you a level of pleasure unlike anything you have ever experienced." How true those words had been. The feeling of him pushing inside her had been dark, delicious, and naughty. The initial burning quickly morphed into the most overwhelming pleasure she'd ever known.

Zach had set a desperate rhythm and pinched her nipples as he'd whispered, "Come when you're ready, kitten." She'd felt her entire body respond to his words and her orgasm washed over her in huge, pounding waves. She heard Alex shout his release at the same time she felt Zach's cock pulsing seed splash against the entrance to her womb. She faintly remembered collapsing onto Zach's chest and his arms wrapping tightly around her before she'd let sleep overtake her. They'd had similar sessions several times since returning home, but none had been as magical as that first night.

Shaking her head and bringing herself back to the moment, Katarina focused on the fact she was finally going to visit The ShadowDance Club as Alex and Zach's submissive and wife. Just thinking about all the possibilities sent her pulse racing. She wasn't sure what they had planned, but it was entirely possible they'd do a public scene. While she didn't consider herself an exhibitionist, the idea of other people watching her husbands fuck her was making her so wet, she was worried she was going to have to go clean up yet again if she didn't get her thoughts back onto something less arousing.

Kat couldn't help smiling to herself when she thought about the special gift she had for them tonight—a small white plastic stick with two pink lines she'd carefully wrapped in pretty paper topped with a silk bow. She planned to give it to them sometime toward the end of the evenings' activities. Knowing how overprotective her husbands could be, she wanted to make sure she got to play at The Club first because she was certain once they knew they were going to be daddies in the spring, she wouldn't be getting another chance anytime soon. Smiling to herself, Kat unconsciously placed her hand protectively over her still-flat stomach and sighed.

ALEX AND ZACH stood just inside the room, watching their beautiful wife lost in thought as she looked out the back windows. Not for the first time, they both thanked God above for the multiple 'second chances' they'd been given with the angel standing before them. Speaking quietly, Zach asked.

"When do you think she plans to tell us?"

They'd known before she did she was pregnant. The two of them knew her body so intimately that even the most subtle change couldn't escape their notice. Hell, even if they hadn't noticed her breasts were more sensitive than usual or that her skin seemed to glow more than before, the way she tended to turn a bit green at times would surely have given her away.

Alex smiled and said, "I don't know, probably tonight. If I know our beautiful wife, she wants to play at The Club before we drop a protective net over her." He chuckled to himself, then added, "How she thought she could keep her body's changes from us baffles me."

"I know. I'm pretty sure she didn't really fall for our story about accidentally forgetting to pack her birth control pills for our honeymoon." He grinned to himself; it had been a stroke of pure genius when they'd told her their honeymoon trip destination was a surprise and to not worry about a thing, they'd pack for her. They'd known for years that Kat's dream was to have a houseful of children, and since they were both more than anxious to make that dream come true, they'd managed to 'forget' those tiny little pills.

"She doesn't even realize she places her hand protectively over our child, hell, even the security guys have noticed and started a 'When is she due?' baby pool. Knowing those jokers, they'll add gender and multiple birth questions, so the damned thing is going to be worth a fortune to the winner by the time she gives birth."

"I'd heard about that and my money is on Grayson. I swear, the man's sixth sense scares the shit out of me sometimes." Alex smiled, then said, "Let's go get our woman, and remember, we aren't going to tip our hand. Let her enjoy surprising us. God knows she's earned every moment of happiness we can ever give her."

"Amen to that, brother. Amen to that."

Chapter 27

A LEX WRAPPED HIS arms around Katarina and turned her toward his chest. He had to smile, submissives were always barefoot while inside The Club, and they'd made certain their sweet little sub also observed that same rule when they were alone in their home. He and his brother were both tall men, and they towered above their diminutive wife. They had chosen her dress for this evening, and the very sheer midnight blue mini was actually little more than long strips of fabric held up by a sparkling ribbon topped with what he'd heard Jenna refer to as spaghetti straps.

Jenna had helped them purchase several club dresses for Katarina before she'd left right after their wedding on what she'd told them would be a several-month, work-related trip abroad. He wasn't sure what had taken place between his sister and Colt that night, but whatever it was, it had been enough to send her hightailing it back to Denver before dawn the next morning. Before they'd landed at their first honeymoon destination, he'd heard she'd been *suddenly called* to check the viability of several locations Lamont Oil was scouting for development in countries all over the world. She was running, no doubt about it. He and Zach had decided they wouldn't get involved unless the situation had a negative impact on Kat.

Now that Kat was carrying their child, she'd need her friend's love and support. He'd call his little sister tomorrow and begin reeling her in.

Thinking of the scene they had planned for her tonight, Alex felt like he was about to burst through his leathers. Tying her to the St. Andrew's Cross in the middle of the main lounge was going to guarantee every member in attendance would be watching. They expected a full house tonight because word had spread quickly that the owners were finally going to publicly claim their woman. Flogging her bare skin with strokes that started as little more than tickles until they sent flaming pulses to her clit was going to be something to behold. Watching her pale back and ass turn pink, then deep red as they sent her in to subspace was sure to have the entire club as mesmerized as they would be.

While she was floating, they'd move to the leather lounger they'd placed off to the side of the stage. The spotlights would glow with soft pink and gold-toned light to highlight her beautiful backside and cascading blonde curls while they fucked her ass and pussy at the same time. They'd spent a lot of their honeymoon preparing her, making sure she'd been properly stretched by the plugs they'd taken along, and the last night of their trip had been a night none of them would ever forget.

Tonight's scene would require them working in tandem, but they would make sure they all climaxed at the same time. They knew the expectations from their members would be high for Katarina's first club appearance, and they'd worked meticulously to make sure no one was disappointed. Bringing himself back to the present, he looked down at the sweet pixie before him and said another prayer of thanks before speaking.

"You look lovely in your club wear, my love." Alex kissed the tip of her nose before handing her off to his brother.

Zach smiled down at her. "Isn't she the most beautiful woman you've ever seen, brother? She looks like an angel, all sparkles and flowing material. This sheer dress shows off her new nipple clamps, too. And that bare pussy, um-hmm-hmm. Heaven on earth for sure."

Kat had finally admitted to them that waxing her 'privates' as she liked to call them, added a whole new dimension of sensation to sex. The night after she'd been waxed at the mini-spa inside The Club, she'd nearly levitated off the bed the first time Zach's tongue had run over her newly bared flesh. Since then, she and spa operator Rissa had become friends and had even met a few times in town for lunch. Rissa had regaled her with tales of all the colorful things she'd heard when ripping wax strips off clients; Kat told them she'd laughed so hard, she'd been afraid she'd pee her pants.

"The nipple clamps are beautiful, thank you for them, by the way. But the diamond clit-clip is making me… um, well, let's say a bit anxious." The way she was looking directly up at him made Zach smile. She wouldn't miss the ways his eyes darkened at her words. Evidently, their sweet wife wanted to play with fire tonight.

Clearing his throat, Zach leaned forward and whispered in her ear, "I know what you're trying to do, and it won't work, kitten. The jewelry stays on, and if you're not careful, you'll find yourself over my lap and your new glass butt plug shoved in that beautiful ass of yours. I can assure you every Dom at the reception would know exactly why you were walking oddly. It might be just the thing to spice up the reception, perhaps we'd have you spend a few minutes bent over, grasping your pretty ankles, so you could show off your earned punishment." Zach chuckled at Kat's reaction to the picture he'd painted in her mind.

Looking at her intently, he could see she was almost panting, the telltale flutters of her pulse at the base of her throat and her dilated eyes clearly indicated her arousal. She was so fucking perfect, it never ceased to amaze him. Looking up at his brother, he knew his wide grin made him look like the lovesick fool he was, and he didn't give a damn.

Alex reached for her and tipped her chin up to meet his gaze.

"Oh yes, love, perhaps you need a little reminder about the discipline this evening is going to require. Hmm, if you're finding your jewelry gifts a bit distracting, a few swats might be just the thing to bring your focus back to your loving Masters."

Zach bit back his laugh because he knew how much Alex loved watching her eyes go from their normal bright, lighter blue to the lust-filled deep sapphire blue they always became when she was aroused. And after Zach's little prep speech, her pupils were so dilated, the light blue color was little more than a narrow ring.

Alex and Zach had spent hours secretly reading everything they could find online about pregnancy and BDSM and knew an erotic spanking was not going to damage her precious cargo. They'd also already seen her increase in responsiveness; oh yes, pregnancy certainly seemed to agree with their lovely bride.

KAT WORRIED HER heart was going to beat itself right out of her chest, she was so turned-on. *Geez, these pregnancy hormones are something to behold.* She knew the joys of an erotic spanking and was sure Alex was right, it would bring her some much needed relief. Ooh, the joy of having husbands who knew her even better than she knew herself. Alex sat down and pulled her over his lap. Their erotic spankings were always given OTK—over the knee. They'd explained how it was more personal and intimate, and she certainly wouldn't argue that point. No siree, her husbands had this pleasure thing down to a fine science. Neither of them seemed to like spankings as a punishment for her, but God knew they could sure think up torturous ways to remind her of the rules—orgasm delay and denial among their favorites—the rat bastards. She reminded them frequently the Bill of Rights was in place to protect her from 'cruel and unusual punishment' but they seemed convinced that amendment didn't apply to not allowing her to orgasm.

"Well, you seem to be quite distracted, love. I've asked you the same question twice, and you have yet to answer me. Having trouble focusing for any particular reason this evening?" If she hadn't known Alex so well, she might have missed the underlying humor in his voice. There was something else, too, but before she could identify it, a slap landed firmly on her ass. Wow, when had they moved her dress—if you could really call it that—aside? Geez, she really was zoning out today.

"Katarina… Focus. Let's review. What is your safe word?" Alex's sharp words finally seemed to penetrate and bring her back into the moment.

"It's red, Sir," Kat answered clearly.

"Good girl. Now, let's see if we can't help you overcome your little distraction problem, so we can all better enjoy our evening." And with that, Alex landed several stinging blows to her rounded ass. He never hit the same place twice in succession, and while they were sharp and certainly were warming her up nicely, they were clearly not meant as punishment.

Zach stood to the side, and Kat would bet he was smiling as his brother spanked her, quickly heating her ass. For two rough, tough former Special Forces soldiers, they sure had become fond of the color pink... at least when it concerned her ass. Before standing Katarina back up, he ran his fingers through her now-soaking-wet pussy, eliciting a sensual moan that felt like it rumbled from the back of her throat.

"Well, Zach, it seems our sweet wife needs a bit more help, what do you say?"

Zach chuckled and pulled her closer. Holy hell, her legs were trembling so much she wondered if they were going to hold her up before he steadied her.

"I'd be happy to help you, kitten. Now, lie across my lap, and let's see if we can't get you to where you need to go." Five sharp swats later, Zach plunged his fingers into her wet heat and said, "Come now, kitten." Those simple words sent Kat sailing over the edge into oblivion.

KAT HAD KNOWN she was almost floating when Zach laid her over his knees, but she'd barely registered the swats before he'd tugged on the clit clip, then pushed through her swollen pussy lips. When she heard his command to come, she'd been launched into space. Time stood still, and the rush of pleasure had been unlike anything she'd ever experienced.

Holy Mother of God, those books were right, sex really was amplified by pregnancy hormones. She didn't even remember them standing her back up or Zach settling her on his lap.

The next thing she was really cognizant of was his softly spoken words of praise and Alex gently cleaning her cream from between her thighs. Their aftercare was always one of her favorite parts of a scene. Even though the orgasms were over-the-top amazing, the cuddling and care afterward made her feel like the most cherished and loved woman in the world.

"I love you both so very much, I just don't even really know how to tell you how happy you make me." Kat looked between both Alex and Zach and saw their love for her reflected clearly in their expressions. Deciding she wanted to give them their gift in private, she continued. "I have something for you, a gift I want to share with you if we have time. I mean, I don't want to change your plans or anything, but this is kind of important, and, well…"

KAT WAS CUT off from continuing by Zach. "We will always make time for you, kitten. What do you have for us?" He had to bite the inside of his mouth to suppress the stupid grin he knew was going to be on his face for the next several months. They'd decided to let her have her moment, and they didn't want to steal her thunder by telling her they already knew about her *gift*.

Alex watched as Katarina moved to the mantle of the

fireplace and picked up a small beautifully wrapped box he hadn't noticed lying in plain sight. It reminded him of a box a bracelet might be displayed in at a jewelry store. Looking at his brother, he could see Zach had the same puzzled expression. Holy shit, had they misread the signs? Christ, they were both going to be disappointed if they'd been wrong. Katarina stood in front of them both.

"This is for both of you, please work together to open it. I hope it's the first of several gifts like it I'll be able to give you." And then she held the box out to them, waiting until they each had a hand on it before she let it go.

KAT WATCHED PUZZLED expressions cross both of their faces and bit her lip. God, she was nervous, what if they weren't happy about the baby? What if they truly had just forgotten her birth control pills when they'd packed her things for the honeymoon? What if they didn't think she'd be a good mother? Oh God, what if they wanted tests to know which of them was the biological father? She really didn't think she could handle that one at all. By the time they'd gotten the box open, she was almost hyperventilating.

"Katarina, love, what is this plastic stick?" Alex was pretty sure both he and his brother knew exactly what the stick was, but he sensed she'd almost worried herself into a full-blown state of panic, so he'd wanted to get her head back in the conversation quickly. It had taken them a couple of minutes to unwrap the box because their fingers had been shaking so much, they'd had trouble dealing with the intricately tied silk bow.

Alex saw Katarina hesitate for a couple of seconds before her words pushed out in a rush. "It's the stick from a pregnancy test. Um, well, I'm, I mean... we, all of us I mean, we're going to be parents. I'm pregnant." Her words had tumbled out so quickly, she hadn't stopped to take a breath, and Alex made a note to look up online and see if that was bad for the baby.

Smiling to himself, he realized just how overprotective they were going to become. And if their little bundle of joy was a girl, he was fairly certain they'd need to start building turrets and a moat right away. They'd need to be ready for any young man who even considered visiting.

Alex and Zach wrapped their arms around Kat. Hugging her, they pressed kisses to her hair, her face, her fingers. They both got down on their knees, moved the strips of her dress to the side, and reverently kissed her flat little tummy where their growing child lay. Zach was the first to speak.

"Kitten, we are both thrilled you are carrying our child. This is by far the best gift we've ever received. We are overjoyed, and know this always, sweet kitten, you are what makes us whole. We'll protect and cherish you for the rest of our lives."

Alex had stood again and from behind her, wrapped her in his strong arms and spoke close to her ear.

"Seeing you growing round with our child is going to be an amazing experience." He had to stop for a moment to get his emotions back under control. "You enchant us, you are the center of our universe, love. We'll spend the rest of our lives making sure you and every child we're blessed with knows how deeply you are loved each and every day. Brother, if you could go out and make our regrets to our guests, then join us in our suite, I believe our wife needs some extra special attention tonight. I don't want to share this special occasion with anyone else. This celebration belongs to the three of us."

Well, damn and double damn, looks like I won't be going to The Club tonight after all.

Books by Avery Gale

The ShadowDance Club
Katarina's Return – Book One
Jenna's Submission – Book Two
Rissa's Recovery – Book Three
Trace & Tori – Book Four
Reborn as Bree – Book Five
Red Clouds Dancing – Book Six
Perfect Picture – Book Seven

Club Isola
Capturing Callie – Book One
Healing Holly – Book Two
Claiming Abby – Book Three

Masters of the Prairie Winds Club
Out of the Storm
Saving Grace
Jen's Journey
Bound Treasure
Punishing for Pleasure
Accidental Trifecta
Missionary Position
Another Second Chance
Star-Crossed Miracles
Dusted Star
Lilly's Choice

The Wolf Pack Series
Mated – Book One
Fated Magic – Book Two
Tempted by Darkness – Book Three

The Knights of the Boardroom
Book One
Book Two
Book Three

The Morgan Brothers of Montana
Coral Hearts – Book One
Dancing with Deception – Book Two
Caged Songbird – Book Three
Game On – Book Four
Well Bred – Book Five

Mountain Mastery
Well Written
Savannah's Sentinel
Sheltering Reagan

Enchanted Holidays
The Christmas Painting

I would love to hear from you!

Website:
www.averygale.com

Facebook:
facebook.com/avery.gale.3

Twitter:
@avery_gale